P9-DMG-859

IN THE RED

ALSO BY ELENA MAULI SHAPIRO

13, rue Thérèse

IN THE RED

A Novel

Elena Mauli Shapiro

Little, Brown and Company
New York Boston London

The characters and events in this book are fictitious. Any similarity to real persons, living or dead, is coincidental and not intended by the author.

Little, Brown and Company
Hachette Book Group
237 Park Avenue, New York, NY 10017
littlebrown.com

First Edition: September 2014

Little, Brown and Company is a division of Hachette Book Group, Inc. The Little, Brown name and logo are trademarks of Hachette Book Group, Inc.

ISBN 978-0-316-40536-2

LCCN 2014940621

10 9 8 7 6 5 4 3 2 1

RRD-C

Printed in the United States of America

For Harris

IN THE RED

At first Irina was scared of colors. She wore the black crayon down to a tiny nub without touching any of the others, outlining amorphous shapes and filling them in, sometimes filling up the entire page. When they would try to hand her one of the colors, she would cry. This is what they told her years later; she didn't remember any of this. She didn't remember that she once spoke Romanian either, though she was already almost five when they adopted her. She didn't speak at all for nearly a year, and then she spoke English. English is when the memories begin.

By then, she was using the colors. Not the red, though; she was still scared of the red. Maybe thinking that if she touched it, it might be flame hot or frozen-metal cold. They never knew what she thought would happen. When they asked her, she shook her head and clammed up. She spoke so little that developmental problems were suspected. The suspicions were dispelled by the speed with which she learned to read. She was just a taciturn little soul, watching the play of other children rather than joining in. Did she consider herself too far above them or too far below? Did they bore her or was she afraid of them? She seldom exhibited temper. She obeyed almost every order, but when she chose not to, her rebellion was silent. A hearing problem was suspected but test results showed she was on the acute side of the normal range.

Sometimes her adoptive father was disturbed by something that looked like mute, expectant pain in her eyes. What she seemed to be waiting for could not be known. The mystery of the pain's source unsettled him more than the pain itself. It was that look she had of waiting for some kind of blow that made him decide that they should tell her she was adopted, that she wasn't born in the United States. Did she remember? She said she remembered nothing, but didn't seem shocked at what he'd told her. Telling her must have helped somehow. At eight years old she must have been old enough to absorb the news and do something with it. It gave her an explanation for the great big blank of the first four years of her life. Maybe she was strange because she wasn't from here. Maybe that was all.

They showed her Romania on a map. It was far. They said it was much smaller and much older than the United States. She stopped her father at the word "older." She wanted to know how one country could be older than another. Was it the same way one person could be older than another?

They found two books for her: a Romanian history and a collection of Romanian fairy tales. She read them both. Because she was alternating reading the fairy tales with reading the history, the two volumes became mashed together in her head. Her native country became for her a place where myth and fact were the same thing. Maybe she had been given the texts too young—or maybe she understood them in a deeper way than if she'd seen them later, when her rational mind was more developed. As an amalgam, the stories coalesced into a kind of sense only she could discern.

Her mother read the books she had given her daughter after it was clear that Irina was quite fascinated by them. She had to wrench the volume of fairy tales loose from her daughter's grasp before she got to look at them. When she was finished with the book, she thought maybe she had made a mistake. She should not have trusted that they would be like the stories she knew where the princess got her prince and lived happily ever after. What had she done, giving a little girl such unremittingly gruesome texts, in which everybody was torn apart and died?

Irina must have been thirteen years old the day she came home from school and whipped past her father into the bathroom faster than he'd thought she could move. She came back out silently brandishing her underwear like the head of a vanquished enemy. It was bloody. She looked, of all things, unfathomably angry. Weren't girls supposed to be happy to become women? He called his wife. She took Irina away to the cocoon of her room to talk about womanly things, sending him out to the store to buy sanitary pads.

After that, Irina started to pick up the habit of disappearing. She would go off on aimless walks for hours, even—especially—when she knew her parents were looking for her. When she was gone, she didn't think of their worry or agitation. She didn't think of them at all in her unmoored space. She liked to drift into forgetfulness; she hated returning to the life she had been given. Her parents' recriminations made her feel awful. She didn't want them to suffer. More importantly, she didn't want to watch them suffer. The only way not to see their suffering, really, was to disappear forever.

It had to be a beautiful day. Late summer in California could be so beautiful. There must have been a bright blue sky naked of clouds, a breeze carrying the scent of invisible flowers over the entire campus. The stately quad was radiant, its sandstone a warm yellow in the sunlight. The palm trees suggested a tropical vacation spot more than a venerable institution of higher learning. The place looked like a postcard.

An enormous surge of new, clever, well-adjusted, good-looking youths flooded campus that day. A convergence of valedictorians, star athletes, music prodigies, math whizzes. Clear complexions, cooperative temperaments, perfect scores on standardized tests, bright futures, impressive careers. Dressed in good clothes but never ostentatious. White, leavened with a gratifying sprinkle of the finest yellow and brown America could provide. The new students would be immediately at home here. Their very first meal at the dorm cafeteria would confront them with a sea of smiling faces, in every direction a new friend. Such fine young citizens away from home for the first time would never slide into loneliness, unsightly binge drinking, crippling bouts of impostor syndrome. Counseling services would not be overwhelmed during the first rush of midterms.

Irina's new room in her new dorm was shaped like a train car, with the door at one end and a window at the other that opened out onto a green field, where the fine young citizens threw Frisbees during the daylight hours or kissed and held hands while looking up at reams of bright stars during the night hours. A closet, a bed, a dresser, a desk, were lined up on each side of the room. Sturdy institutional furniture, each side of the room mirroring the other. Her roommate had arrived before her and piled all her things on the right-hand bed. Left would be Irina's side.

Later, after all the unpacking, the right side of the room would feature an ironic lava lamp and a couple of large posters from the university bookstore: a favorite band performing in a stadium, a French Impressionist painting. Pictures of parents, a brother, a dog, pinned over a desk lamp. There would be a worn stuffed tiger tucked into the bed like a tiny sleeping person, the comforter just covering its round, high belly where some cotton batting was starting to leak out of a side seam. The left side of the room would lack such personal touches. A lamp, a computer, a blue bedspread, all new and untouched as if they had come directly from the big-box store where they were purchased. The bare white wall suggested an identity completely indifferent to announcing itself with either borrowed art or family photos. It was as if Irina were staying in a hotel, as if someone opening her dresser drawer might find only a Bible left there by the Gideons instead of her neatly folded clothes.

White plastic glow-in-the-dark stars had been stuck all over the ceiling by the pair of girls who'd occupied the room the previous year. In the daylight, they were easy to miss on the white ceiling, which was why maintenance had neglected to take them down over the summer. But Irina noticed them right away, noticed the implied friendship of last year's unseen girls who were somewhere on the campus right now, starting their second year.

When Irina arrived, her roommate was not there. Only her things were in the room. Irina went to run campus errands—picking up her student ID card, getting a box at the post office—without having met her. When she returned to the dorm, the rest of the afternoon was a blur of where-are-you-from-what-did-you-get-on-the-SAT-do-you-like-your-roommate-what's-your-major-what-classes-are-you-taking-what-kind-of-music-do-you-like. So many faces and names, it was hopeless to try to remember anybody. She would, in time. She would differentiate all eighty-five dorm mates, somehow. She would recognize their shoes under the stall partitions in the bathroom. She would recognize their voices while they squealed in drunken glee outside her door at 2 a.m. the night before an exam. She would recognize their smiles when they received a good grade, a package from home, flowers on Valentine's Day. She spoke to them little, but she watched them attentively.

Back in the train-car room, the roommate was there, on the phone, talking loudly to the lanky brother whose face Irina would know from a family photograph.

The roommate shouted, as if the connection was bad, "Okay, bye, you have a great time there at the Stanford of the East!"

After hanging up, she explained to Irina, "He told me to have a good time out here at the Harvard of the West."

Irina nodded, gave a tight smile, and offered her hand to the girl to shake. The two girls were awkward with each other immediately, and would remain so the entire year. There was something about Irina that put the other girl off. Something about the stark contrast between her long, loosely curly black hair and the pallor of her skin. Or maybe her slow, uncomfortable smile. Something about Irina forbade chumminess, keeping the two girls at a distance with a faintly crackling tension in it, like a high-voltage power line.

The first day of the school year was supposed to end with the new roommates chatting themselves happily to sleep about where they had come from and where they intended to go, but for Irina it ended in silence tinged with preemptive disappointment. It wouldn't be different this time; Irina was not suddenly good at making friends just because she had gone away to college. The plastic stars on the ceiling glowed softly in the darkened room.

September at the university was warmer than Irina had expected. Those who knew the area called it an Indian summer. Those from other parts of the country wondered if fall would ever come. To get away from the confusing youthful buzz of the dorm, Irina walked to the adjoining town on a weekday afternoon when she had no class. She looked into shop windows, strolling slowly along the sunny street. There were few people. In the courtyard of a bookstore that had formerly been a movie theater, there was a small fountain. The water glittered like an invitation. Irina took off her sandals and sat on the edge of the fountain, dipping her feet in. The slight shock of the cool water made a pleasant shiver run through her. She gazed at the Italian tile work under her submerged feet, losing herself in the bright, tiny squares.

"Does that help?"

She looked up at the source of the voice. A man was standing there looking at her with his hands in his pockets and the sleeves on his white linen shirt rolled up to his elbows. "I'm sorry?" she answered, though she might have preferred not to.

"Does it help against the heat, to sit with your feet in the water like that?"

She shrugged. It would be best to ignore him, but she couldn't look away from his eyes. They were so dark that she couldn't quite tell the irises from the pupils, as if he were looking out at her through two vortices. She watched him untie his shiny black leather shoes and ball up his socks inside them. He rolled the cuffs of his slacks to just below his knees and sat next to her. She stared at his bare feet next to hers in the shimmering water. He had tawny skin, delicate bones. She considered picking up her sandals and running away.

"I am sorry. I am very forward. But are you, perhaps, Romanian?"

"No," she answered, before she had time to be surprised at the question.

"Ah. It's just that…you look like a girl from the old country. You have a Romanian face."

What precisely about her face was Romanian? How could she resist this observation? She had to relent, had to allow him to reel her in at least a little bit. "Well, I'm of Romanian origin."

"Oh? What is your name?"

"Irina Greene."

"Greene? You must be Romanian through your mother."

"I was adopted by Americans."

"So you were born there."

There was a silence while the idea of Irina not having been born an American hung in the warm air between her and the strange man. If Irina were older, she might have said that he was undressing her with his eyes. But she was young enough to know that what he was doing was entirely more alarming than that. He said, "I was in the eastern side of your country this summer, and I heard a sound there that I had never heard before. Have you ever heard cicadas?"

"No, we don't have them out west."

"We don't have them where I come from either. It was prodigious, like a jungle sound. I had to ask people what it was. They said that it was the insect's mating call. Only the males make this sound."

"The females don't say anything?"

"Yes, they are silent. When they are receptive they flick their wings. Then afterward they lay eggs in tree bark. When the eggs hatch, the nymphs fall and burrow in the ground and come up seventeen summers later. To live only a few weeks during which they do not eat, only fuck. And once they do they all die. There were little rotting shells all over the place. They will dissolve into the earth to feed their brood."

"Yes, but in English you can only dissolve into a liquid. Decompose, more like."

He gave her an evaluating once-over. "Ah, you are clever, I see."

"Sorry," she answered tartly.

He laughed and said, "Don't worry. Being clever is forgivable when you are so pretty to look at."

He laughed some more at the look she gave him, flashing his perfect teeth. She didn't know what to think of him, whether she found him interesting or completely ridiculous or frightening or all these things at once. He made it difficult to think when he wore his shirt with the top two buttons undone like that. She wanted to put her face there and peer at what was inside. "Are you a student at the university here? You look almost too young."

"I skipped a grade."

"What does this mean?"

"It means I didn't go to fourth grade. They put me in fifth grade after third."

"Then you are *very* clever."

Irina shrugged. "Maybe," she said, attempting to cover her growing embarrassment with worldliness. "Fourth is a fairly disposable grade. What's your name?"

Still smiling, the man spoke with mock solemnity. "I am Andrei Vadrescu. I was born the Gypsy bastard of the village whore, and now I am a respectable American entrepreneur. Pleased to meet you, Irina Greene. Very pleased to meet you."

When he extended his hand, she had no choice but to take it. When he offered her a ride back to her dorm, she had no choice but to accept, though it wasn't the sort of thing she would normally do, get in some strange man's car. What called her there? The air-conditioned chill inside his nearly soundless luxury sedan? What made her ask him, on the drive back, to tell her a story?

"What sort of story?" he asked pleasantly.

"Tell me a Romanian story."

Zece

Once upon a time something happened. Had it not happened, it would not be told. At the end of the winding trail, at the foot of the high green mountains, three shepherds tended their flocks. One of them was Ungurean, the other Vrancean, and the last Moldavian. The Moldavian was the handsomest and richest of the three. The other two were jealous that he had the finest flocks with the softest, whitest wool; the biggest, most beautiful dog, bigger than the sheep, even, with shining, alert eyes; and the finest, most beautiful horse, all black with a white star on his forehead, who was more finely muscled and could gallop faster than any steed of the royalty. The Ungurean and the Vrancean plotted in their rotted hearts to kill the Moldavian and split his possessions among themselves.

They thought about it for many days. Then, one cold, clear night, they met in the darkness and they agreed to stalk the Moldavian every evening while the sun died on the horizon. They would hide in the trees and wait for the big guard dog to leave the man's side. When the man was finally alone, they would take him from behind and slit his throat. They did not know that in the bushes behind them was a tiny lamb who heard what they had decided, and this lamb was the Moldavian's favorite. The lamb's name was Miorița. She was the smallest of all the lambs, with the softest, whitest wool, a little black snout, and big orange eyes.

For three days, the Vrancean and the Ungurean hid in the trees with their blades ready to cut the Moldavian when the sky darkened, but the big fierce dog did not leave the man's side. For all three of these days, the lamb bleated sadly until her voice cracked and almost broke. On the third day, her master came to her and said, What is the matter, little Miorița? Are you sick? Is the grass bitter? Don't be scared of wolves; the hound will keep them off.

No, master, the little lamb said, it's much worse than that. Don't let your big brave dog leave your side when the sun sets. Every night when it gets dark, the Ungurean and the Vrancean mean to murder you. They wait for the hound to leave so they can strike.

Sweet lamb Miorița, the dog must leave my side sometime, and if what you say is true, then my days are over. Tell the two of them to let my bones lie here on this hill and let my blood soak into this earth to feed this grass, so that I'll always be here with my flock. And if anyone should ask after me, don't say I am dead. Tell them…a beautiful story.

The next night, one of the sheep got lost as it was getting dark. The dog left the man's side to go look for the sheep. The Moldavian sat on a rock and did not move. He watched the sun dissolve into the beautiful green hills. He waited as the Ungurean and the Vrancean came up behind him. They put their hands over his face and cut his throat and he died very quickly and almost without pain. After that, the killers took the possessions of the murdered man—but the horse and the dog ran away, for they would serve no one but their master. The lamb Mioriţa ran away also, and when she left the flock, the whole lot of sheep was taken by a plague that rotted their hides and poisoned their meat. The disease spread through the flocks of both men, and they wound up with nothing. They were too ashamed to go back to the village for having lost their wealth, so they died of hunger up in the mountains.

The lamb Mioriţa had many adventures on the way home, to the Moldavian's native village. She went to the house where the shepherd had been born, to his old mother with a yellow scarf over her gray hair and a rough wool girdle. The mother recognized the little lamb's bright orange eyes and said, Mioriţa, why have you left my son's flock?

Dear Mama, your son's flock was dispersed to the four winds.

Has something bad happened to my boy?

No, dear Mama. A beautiful pale princess with fiery hair like the setting sun passed through the hills in her royal carriage and saw your beautiful son, slim as a willow leaf; and his dear face, fair as the moon; and his curly hair, black as a crow's feather; and his bright eyes, blue as a summer day. She fell in love with him at once and took him as her bridegroom, to go back to her kingdom, where they would reign together. They were married that very night. The mountain was their priest, the birds were the fiddlers, and the sun and the moon came down to hold your dear son's bridal crown. The stars were the torches, and a bright one fell from the sky that night to bless their union.

Oh, dear Miorița, the mother said with tears in her eyes, my son has been blessed, and I saw his star fall that night. I hope he will come again one day to show me his splendor and the children not of this earth that the princess will bear him.

Perhaps he will, dear Mama, but he will be very busy with affairs of the state, and he lives so far away.

The mother accepted Miorița's answer and took in the little lamb. They lived a quiet life together. Every night the mother would sit and hope her son's royal carriage would come rolling into the village. She watched the bright orange sunset, thinking of the fiery hair of the beautiful princess, waiting for stars to fall.

Andrei didn't waste any time. After he told Irina the story, he stole a kiss from her. She had just released her seat belt and let it snake itself open across her; she was about to say thank you and good-bye when he leaned swiftly across the car. The shock of his tongue in her mouth made her raise both hands as if she had the flickering notion that she would push him away. Instead she braced herself as if for a crash, one palm pressed against the coolness of the windowpane.

It was her first kiss. He had her cornered. He must have known it would be a fortunate gamble. Clearly the newness of the experience had its charm, given how Irina's back arched to meet Andrei's hand when he reached for her breast. It was a disaster. Irina had been trying to believe that she was an intelligent, rational person, and now this. How much would it have cost her to turn her face away? How much did it cost her not to?

Andrei had two associates, Dragos Popescu and Vasilii Grigoriev. Dragos was stocky and bald but not too bad to look at. He had a brutal charm. Every week he brought around a different girl, always a quiet girl with a soft, hazy look from the drugs he gave her. That was part of his attraction, certainly, his generosity with substances that made girls forget. Irina could tell that Vasilii disapproved of these sorts of relations. He never acknowledged the girls in any way, never let his limpid eyes pause on them. He did not mind Irina; she earned from him a vaguely benevolent indifference. He spoke so little that it was not obvious what he was doing with Andrei and Dragos in the first place. When the two of them conferred in Romanian he was just as lost as Irina was, yet they treated him with a hushed respect. He never brought any girls around. He had long, pretty hands like a pianist. He had been in the Soviet Army.

Irina liked the sound of Romanian. It sounded like an offspring of Italian and Russian. If she closed her eyes and let her mind drift while Andrei and Dragos talked, she could perhaps summon something familiar about the language's melody, like a song she'd heard long ago, the lyrics forgotten. But Dragos didn't like her listening. Once he turned to her midconversation with Andrei; it took her a few seconds to realize that the Romanian that was coming out of him was suddenly aimed at her. The tone was hectoring. She couldn't tell what he wanted. She put her palms up and shrugged to indicate that she didn't understand, that she surrendered. He eyeballed her across the table. "So, none of what I said—nothing of it means anything to you?"

"None of it."

"So explain this to me, how you are a Romanian who does not understand Romanian."

"I never said I was Romanian."

Andrei glanced between Irina and Dragos, who remained unconvinced. Vasilii took a slow sip of his vodka and said quietly, "Leave the girl alone. Get another drink."

There was nothing further to say on the subject after that. She would often feel Dragos looking at her, evaluating how one could possibly be and not be a thing at the same time. There was something satisfying about the tingle of his mistrust, about being an unresolved issue to a man of consequence in the world.

For now it was back to the business at hand, and the business switched to English. Dragos started to tell a story. Irina watched his red, wry face as he spoke with rollicking amusement. He was getting loud enough that Irina worried that the barkeep would overhear, would associate her with this boisterous man who liked to tell stories to his friends in public places about sad, fat girls who sucked him off in his car though he knew he would never see them again. "I do not know why she offered," he said. "I gave no sign that I liked her."

"That's because you are such a prize," Andrei said. "She was making a last-ditch effort to acquire you."

"Ah, she probably thought I would give her more pills, the poor thing."

They both laughed while Vasilii looked on in neutral silence. Dragos took a swig of his vodka. "I should have said no," he sighed, "but—I didn't."

"Since when do you give a shit about *should?*" Andrei quipped.

Dragos looked straight at Irina as he said, "You can't say no to a young one, even if she is fat. Even when they are fat, the young ones are taut. And that is why we like them so much, isn't it, Andrei?"

"Long live the smooth skin and the taut flesh. I will drink to that."

"The firmness is nice, but it is not what is most lovely about young ones," Vasilii said quietly, his voice stopping Andrei in the midst of raising his glass.

Vasilii stirred the ice in his drink. He watched the cubes jostle as they rang gently against the glass.

"Well?" Andrei said.

"What?"

"Won't you tell us what is most lovely, then?"

Vasilii took his time summoning his answer, tapping his stirrer against the rim of his glass and putting it down on the table. "What is so lovely about them is that they will take the shape of whatever container you choose to put them in, like water."

"Grigoriev, you poet, what the hell does this mean?" Dragos laughed.

"It means a woman who has been around, who may have pushed people out of herself, who may have realized that the world does not end when there is no man in the house, that a woman with lines on her face and hip bones that have been creaked apart by growing life will not go breathless with the need to give you what you want. The young ones are so good, my prosaic friend, because they will say: Do you like me in this dress? Would you think me prettier blonde? Shall I put bags of silicone in my tits? Shall I be your toy? Would this please you? There is no limit to how much they will cut themselves to please you. You should be grateful, Popescu, to all their papas for not loving them."

This observation amounted to possibly the most words Irina had ever heard Vasilii string together in one utterance, more words than she'd heard come out of him in an entire week. For all she knew, Andrei and Dragos had never heard so much at once out of him either. They did look suitably surprised.

"Vasilii," Andrei said, "this is what Dragos's cocksucking stories make you think of?"

Vasilii did not answer. Instead, all three of them looked at Irina, like animals on the hunt who had caught a promising scent on the wind. The predatory looks should have put her off. Should have disgusted her, even. In some recessed place, they might have. But what she felt at that moment was intensely alive, as if their collective gaze was what was warming her blood rather than her tiny, careful sips of vodka.

Were they expecting her to say something? She could not speak. Anything she might have said would have sounded laughably foolish anyway. She watched the three men raise their glasses with a solemnity that she could not read either as joking or genuine. The clink of their toast sounded harsh and jarring. After, they gazed dreamily into what was left of their drinks.

Andrei owned several factories back in Romania that manufactured Western luxury goods. Handbags, clothes, watches—things with logos and signature designs. He also owned other factories not too far away from his legitimate factories that manufactured the counterfeits of those same things, the knockoffs people wear when they want to pretend that they, too, have money. The copies were assembled from the original patterns swiped from or sold by the factories that made the genuine article, with less care and cheaper materials. More importantly, they lacked the serial number that guaranteed the realness of the item in question. Sometimes that number was the only difference between real and fake.

The workers lived in dorms on the premises. There were cafeterias and general stores, entire towns and economies assembled so that they never had to leave the company compound. The workers sent money they earned back home to their families. Families they saw on holiday once, maybe twice a year. Irina used to ask herself, Does Andrei exploit these people? Or is he giving them a chance at a less abject life? Sometimes she would think of them asleep in their gray concrete block buildings while she drifted off on the twin extra-long mattress in her own dorm at night. Except at the hour she was falling asleep they were probably already at work the next morning, right at that moment, in the breaking daylight halfway across the world.

The whole province was famous for these factories. On clear days, distant mountains could be seen cutting up the horizon. The workers were paid the kind of low wages Westerners cannot comprehend as acceptable to any person. Where they are, it is enough to live on. Of course, many of the goods they sewed together fell off the back of the truck. There was a brisk trade between factories: a crate of handbags for a rack of coats. Watches for wallets. Shoes for suitcases. In the whole province, everyone wore what everyone made: items that cost as much as the average Westerner's monthly mortgage payment, worn by people who didn't make enough in a day to buy the Westerner's morning coffee.

This was the sort of thing that Andrei found hilarious, the poor bastards playing dress-up with our bullshit status symbols, with only the dimmest understanding of what they had on their backs. Maybe a little bit of pride, because they saw these things on imported television shows, the American English dubbed over. Irina asked him once if it bothered him that they stole, if he'd ever thought of taking measures against it. He shrugged. "As far as I know, the managers do punish them when they catch them. But sometimes they don't catch them if they get an envelope full of money. Like I give a shit—you know, it is a marginal cost. It does not cut into my profits. We just make their wages lower accordingly."

"You mean if they didn't steal, you would pay them more?"

He thought about it for a second. "No, probably not."

"Andrei?"

"Yes?"

"Do you think these people—do you think they can be happy?"

He laughed then, with uproarious delight. Even when his laughter was unkind he was beautiful in his mirth. Thrilling like the glinting flash of a knife blade you hadn't known was there.

"Darling," he said, "I love it so much that you can ask such a question. But darling, I cannot possibly care whether these fucking peasants whose shithead children threw rocks at me and called me thief because I have dark Gypsy skin—I cannot bring myself to give a shit whether they are happy. They sweat money for those who are stronger and more clever than they are—that is what they do and what they have always done."

He understood the world so neatly. He had a kind of gift, a kind of elemental affinity with the way things are. He simply accepted and played along. And Irina, his little woman, Irina was the one left to brood and wonder whether her parents were somewhere in his factories. Her first parents, the ones whose image had been erased.

Sometimes when he was burrowed all the way inside her he would suddenly pull out almost entirely, just to hear her gasp and watch her face seize with helpless distress, her eyes filling with tears. More like a child being abandoned than a woman being fucked. Was it because she was so young? But she wasn't the first he'd had that young, and none of the others were like this. He'd hover there while she looked up at him with her mouth slightly open, her breath held and her back arched, her whole body perfectly still, waiting for him to decide. He'd plunge in again to the hilt and she'd sob as she parted for him. Sometimes a tear would run down the side of her face, sometimes not. When he whispered in her ear, "I'm here. I'm here," the expression in her gleaming eyes filled his thrumming heart with happiness and terror.

When Irina called her parents the morning before the wedding she had to look up the weather at her university so she would have something to talk to them about. Only a month into her studies, she was already cutting several days of classes to travel to sleazy places with sleazy men. She should have felt shame, but she felt only surprise at finding herself here. So it made a kind of sense that after all this time not bringing a single girl around, Vasilii would marry the first one he let his associates lay eyes on.

"Marriage is an honorable estate," the officiant recited. "It is not to be entered into lightly or unadvisedly, but discreetly and soberly. Into this relationship these two persons come now to be joined. I therefore charge both of you that if you know any reason why you should not be joined in marriage, you make it known at this time."

The officiant looked at the bride and groom and then glanced over at Irina, Dragos, and Andrei in case they had something to say. So far, they'd had not a word for the willowy blonde Vasilii had brought to the business meeting in Las Vegas, an unexpected addition to the large, plush hotel suite they were staying in. Before his associates or Irina could talk to her or even take a good look at her, Vasilii called a limousine to drive them up the strip to the Little White Wedding Chapel, where he would bind his young bride to him.

The officiant was dressed in a gray suit that didn't call attention to itself, while Vasilii was dressed in a much more expensive and better-fitting version of the same thing. The girl did not wear white, and her distracted look made Irina wonder if she quite understood the proceedings. She had on a cherry-blossom shade of pink that brought out the creamy pallor of her skin. The dress had a full skirt with a tulle overlay that reached below the knees, as if she had modeled her outfit on the way American movies represented high school dances in the halcyon 1950s. A wrap of the same tulle as the skirt overlay was slipping off her frail shoulders. She'd somehow found a pair of high-heeled, round-toed shoes in the same shade—possibly dyed to match. She wore no jewelry save for a pair of large diamond studs that must have been false, given the homeliness of the clothes. Unless Vasilii had given them to her. Then they were real.

She looked indecently young next to her groom. Was she the same age as Irina? Could she possibly be younger?

"Vasilii Grigoriev, will you take Elena Lukowskaia to be your wedded wife, to live together in the bonds of marriage? Will you love her, comfort her, honor and keep her, so long as you both shall live?"

"I will," Vasilii answered, his gaze on the upturned face of his wide-eyed bride.

"Elena Lukowskaia, will you take Vasilii Grigoriev to be your wedded husband, to live together in the bonds of marriage? Will you love him, comfort him, honor and keep him, so long as you both shall live?"

Vasilii leaned into Elena's ear and whispered something. For a moment she beheld him with an expression that looked as if she were bracing herself to leap into a pool of water she suspected was very cold. But she was not one to stand on the edge for very long. "I will," she said.

At either corner of the podium, behind the officiant, were two white wicker stands piled high with pink flowers. The flowers were cloth, and a touch dusty. The officiant's voice droned, "Vasilii, repeat after me: 'I, Vasilii...'"

Vasilii repeated. He held the girl's hand. Looking at them, Irina saw that they both had long fingers, delicate wrists—male and female versions of the same hands.

"'...take thee, Elena, to be my wedded wife...'"

Elena's fine, dark blonde hair was cut just below her ears, where it curled under. The broadness of her cheekbones left no doubt that she was a Slav.

"'...to have and to hold from this day forward...'"

"Elena, Irina," Andrei whispered into Irina's ear. "Her name is almost like yours."

Irina turned to look at him. She could not read the distant, dreamy look on his face.

"'...for better or worse, for richer or poorer...'"

Did he mean she'd be next? That *he* would marry *her*?

"'...in sickness and in health, to love and to cherish...'"

Certainly not.

The officiant turned to the girl. "Elena, please repeat after me..." The girl repeated, slowly and carefully, promising to take Vasilii as her wedded husband. Her accent was very thick. Did she understand the words, or was she repeating them phonetically?

"She is just your age," Andrei felt compelled to tell Irina.

Vasilii slipped a plain yellow gold circlet around Elena's finger. When he uttered the words "With this ring I thee wed, and with all my love I thee endow," Irina felt a hot wave wash over her. She was quite certain all of them were doomed, like horses with broken legs, about to be shot.

The officiant did not even seem to be fully conscious when he recited, "Inasmuch as you have thus consented together in marriage, by virtue of the authority vested in me by the laws of the state of Nevada, I now pronounce you husband and wife. You may kiss the bride."

Vasilii took Elena by the waist and drew her to him, and Irina realized then that she had never seen Vasilii take possession of anyone or anything like that, with the happy impatience of one finally putting his hands on an object long awaited. Even when he drank his vodka, he did so slowly and with a kind of apathy, as if he were indifferent to the taste in his mouth. But this girl, she had his attention. She let him tip her back; she opened her mouth for his kiss. A kiss that might have been their first, for all Irina knew. Where did he get this girl?

Afterward, Elena's hand went up to her mouth as a florid blush overtook her face, as if she meant to cover lipstick she knew he had smudged.

In the parking lot, Vasilii showed Elena the marriage license, in the Latin script she quite possibly could not read. As they looked over the page, their two blond heads were close together, nearly touching, her hair's shade as warm as honey and his lightening into white. Irina could not hear what he said to her, but she could see him pause, his finger poised over the page, when he could not think of a word straightaway. He was translating for his bride. Would he explain every word, or might he skip some? The intimacy of their Russian stung Irina with jealousy. She'd never be able to address Andrei in his native tongue like that. Not that he wanted her to. When she'd asked him to teach her, he'd waved her off, saying, "You don't want to speak the shit language of my shit country anyway. You do not need it." She assumed it was because he did not want her to understand his business with Dragos.

But maybe there was some other reason. Maybe it was in the way he said that the shit country was *his*. Not hers, though she had been born there.

That evening, the men stayed in the suite to do business with some guests, sending Irina and Elena out onto the strip to entertain themselves. The sky was growing dimmer, but there was no drop in the staggering heat. In this heat, a breeze did not alleviate the air's weight but only made it worse. How could a desert evening feel so smothering? Maybe it was the excess of bodies holding down the heat over the asphalt, the blast of the freeway-like traffic. The rows of glinting cars ticking with impatience at every traffic light made crossing the street a menacing proposition. It made Irina want to hold Elena's hand, as if she were a defenseless child. Was this nightmarish cacophony of light and sound the first Elena was seeing of America? Irina had never been assaulted by anything like it.

Rolling walkways conveyed clusters of sweaty tourists from

the bustling sidewalk into giant hotel-casino complexes, each themed after a caricature of some time and place. Renaissance Italy. Ancient Egypt. Paris. New York. The circus. The strip's microcosm throbbed in the night. If money corrupted the world, then this was the world that corrupted money. Irina pointed out a cluster of stylized skyscrapers to Elena and attempted an observation in slow, careful English: "This one is supposed to look like New York. See the tiny Empire State Building? It has a whole amusement park in there. With a roller coaster."

Elena gave Irina a drowning look. Irina made a sine curve in the air with her finger. "A roller coaster," she said. "A ride for fun. Do you want to go in and ride it?"

Elena shook her head. "I do not like high up," she said.

"How about we go in this one?" Irina asked, pointing to an enormous fairy-tale castle with turrets topped with colors as bright as children's blocks. Elena nodded and they wended their way in. The wall of climate control that hit them upon entering made Irina gasp. Elena shivered. She was wearing a lot less than she had at the wedding: after the ceremony she'd changed into a frilly red tube top and a flouncy skirt that barely covered her entire rump.

"How do you feel when people look at you?" Irina asked, gesturing up and down the girl's scant outfit. Irina's uncertainty that she was being understood gave her a strange type of freedom to say whatever was on her mind. Elena did not take offense at the question; she merely shrugged.

The slot machines rang merrily. There were suits of armor propped up in the corners, and staff in skimpy costumes meant to suggest medieval clothes moving through the aisles with underwater slowness. The whole place had the feel of being submerged. Hermetic climate, no visible exits, aquarium lighting. The department stores Irina frequented back home were much like this, and they had the same basic purpose. This was the same thing on a grander scale, a monumental mall. Surely, then, it was only the scale that was sinister, that suffused the place with faint alarm. The two girls walked absently through the maze.

Suddenly they were standing before a large, spotlessly clean bas-relief of perfect ancient Egyptians in vibrant color. They must have been conveyed from one casino to the next through some suspended passageway they had no memory of crossing. Now the waiters were wearing white loin wraps and lamé accoutrements, their eyes jarringly stark in their kohl outlines, complete with little fish tails at the temples. "Want to gamble?" Irina asked.

The Russian looked at her with intense focus. "What means 'gamble'?"

Irina took a quarter out of her wallet, parked the two of them in front of one humming slot machine among the din of them, put the quarter in, and pulled the lever. The three displays whirred and clicked into place one by one. Two pairs of cherries and some kind of peach-like fruit. The machine vibrated and then emitted a fierce series of tinny dings in a rollicking melody of joy. It dispensed two quarters into the receiving tray.

"Ha!" Elena said.

"We won!" Irina smiled as Elena scooped one of the quarters from the tray and immediately fed it back into the machine, yanking the lever with great gusto. A bunch of grapes. A jackpot logo. A pair of cherries.

They waited for the machine to sing at them, but it remained silent. Undeterred, Elena put in the second quarter. Again, nothing. She looked at Irina expectantly. Irina was rooting around in her bag for another quarter when a voice shouted, "Hey!"

They looked up. The man striding toward them was not wearing lamé or a pharaonic headdress with a snake on it. He had on a black suit and an earpiece. "Hey you! How old are you?"

The two girls did not even look at each other before they started to run. They lost the man quickly; he probably didn't care enough to really give them chase. It took them long minutes of panting panic to find their twisting way back onto the street. The sky had gotten completely black in the time they'd been inside.

"Why did he ask how old?" Elena said, tugging down her skirt, which had ridden up while she was running.

"In America, you have to be twenty-one to play these games."

"Oh," she said. "But these games, they look like they are for children."

Irina laughed. "Yes, children who feed these games entire mortgage payments one quarter at a time."

"What is '*mortgage*'?"

Irina walked with Elena, trying to explain to her the concept of a homeowner's debt to a bank. Elena could not understand because Irina kept piling her explanation with words Elena had never heard before. Irina gave up. This concept was not important anyway. The two of them were too young to talk about adult debts, about sinking into the red to find a place in the world. But then again, they were certainly too young to be married, and Elena was as of that afternoon. They were too young for all of it, too young even to feed money to dumb machines.

Irina once asked Andrei what was the strangest thing about America when he got here? He said the choice. He noticed the language; the climate; the unknown plants; the inexplicable rituals and behavior of the natives; the way they shook hands with only two fast pumps and then let go immediately; their oversized straight white teeth; the way they spoke louder than necessary; the way the men sat with their legs crossed at the ankles to take up the most room possible, as if their generously sized genitals needed room to breathe; the way advertising could not be escaped; the way money was everywhere; the insincere friendliness; the forgetfulness; the way everything was so quickly and easily forgotten—he said he could get used to all those things. But it was choice that drew him, that was strangest of all.

When he first arrived, he developed a fascination with supermarkets, the miraculous excess of well-organized foods. The way people shuffled bleary-eyed through the aisles tipping brightly colored packaged goods into their carts without any seeming awareness that this was unusual, this was unprecedented in human history, this was almost obscene. The foods for children interested him—what was a blue raspberry? How could a chocolate spread be "part of a nutritious breakfast"? Why did the cheese come in soft flat orange squares in cellophane, unrecognizable and scentless? Scentless—that was strange too, everything so clean. You could not smell the meat, the fish, sometimes not even the fruit. How could you have an entire table covered in peaches not one arm's length away from you and not be able to smell a thing? The glossy skin of the flawless apples made him lay his finger on them to check that they were not fake, not made of wax.

"They are wax," Irina tried to explain when he told her about the apples. "I mean, they are coated with a patina of wax. To make them look that way."

He told her he almost fainted once in the cereal aisle. An entire wall of cardboard boxes screaming at him. Flakes or pellets. Shaped like tiny doughnuts or tiny waffles. Chocolate, neon fruit, peanut butter, marshmallows. Endorsed by athletes, cartoon toucans, ethnically diverse children. Chex, Frosted Flakes, Cheerios, Rice Krispies, Froot Loops, Life, Life, *Life!* He started to breathe fast. How many different kinds of crunchy sweetened grain could one civilization need? How was it possible to pick one out of such a lineup? Was this glut not a harbinger of retribution, disaster? He put his hand on his chest to slow his heart. He looked into the crazed eyes of a cartoon squirrel. He needed some air. He walked briskly outside.

"What I had forgotten," he said with ironic amusement, "was that in August in Las Vegas there is no air. The oven heat punched my chest and I gasped. Like a woman who had just been grabbed by an unseen hand in the dark, I gasped and I reached for something to steady myself. A signpost. Scorching hot in the desert sun. At that moment I could have sworn I heard a little hiss like a drop of oil in the fire. I pulled my hand away and started to laugh. I doubled over and laughed and all the housewives who were loading their cars blasting air conditioners; they must have thought I was barking mad. Irina, I *was* barking mad."

He was smiling as if this was all very funny, but there was still something in his eyes that made her want to hold him. His vulnerability distressed her a thousand times more than her own.

"But I got their nice white teeth, see? No more peasant teeth for me," Andrei said nearly in a whisper. She hadn't known until then that he had caps. She'd never thought of questioning someone's teeth before. She was about to say something when he asked her how old she was when Ceauşescu was shot.

Irina tried to think of the answer to this unexpected question. But it wasn't a number he wanted from her.

He was from the country she had been born in but couldn't remember. She had been born in the place he had run away from, and raised in the place he had run to. Both places he hated and loved. Was the thing he reached for inside her the same thing she reached for inside him?

Andrei answered his own question. "Oh, you must have been only a little slip of a thing. Probably you did not yet speak. Or if you spoke, what you spoke was not English. There is a video of it, you know. But it made me feel, what do you call it? It made me feel shortchanged. You hold out your hand waiting for more, and more does not come. We were cheated. We did not get to watch the bullets go in. We did not get to see them bleeding out. I would have liked to see."

What could she do then except kiss him? It was always the best thing to do when she had no answer. When there was no answer, the only thing to do was revert to skin.

Nouă

The televised grain of the image is faded into the yellow range. Everyone's skin is rendered in a raw orange. This is the revolution. This is the trial. Stern men in military uniforms sit at tables in a barren room in a schoolhouse. Their mouths are set into hard, narrow lines. It must be the camera that fails to capture the glee in their eyes—the promise of blood. But then again, the camera glances over a man in a suit fussily looking at his fingernails, as if he is, after all, indifferent to the promise of blood.

The dictator and his wife sit to be judged in their own little corner, behind an institutional table from which a teacher not long ago asked the children to recite multiplication tables, pledge allegiance to the party. Today the glorious leader and his consort have the dim hollow faces of doomed animals. Like horses with broken legs, about to be shot. The prosecutors say: destruction of state buildings, undermining the economy. They say: crimes against the people, genocide. Did you hear the charges? Have you understood?

I do not answer; I will only answer questions before the Grand National Assembly. I do not recognize this court. The charges are incorrect, and I will not answer a single question here.

This is how the Ceauşescus try to hang on to the shreds of their authority. It must be cold in the room. They keep their coats on. The dictator's hat rests on the table near his wife's purse. He chops at the air with his hand when he tries to make a point.

I repeat: I am the president of Romania and the commander in chief of the Romanian Army. I am the president of the people. I will not speak with you provocateurs anymore, and I will not speak with the organizers of the putsch and with the mercenaries. I have nothing to do with them.

Please, make a note: Ceauşescu does not recognize the new legal structures of power of the country. He still considers himself to be the country's president and the commander in chief of the army. Why did you ruin the country? Why did you export everything? Why did you starve the people?

I will not answer this question. It is a lie that I made the people starve. A lie, a lie in my face.

He looks at the prosecutor. The prosecutor is not deterred. The prosecutor says, We have seen your villa on television, the golden plates from which you ate, the foodstuffs that you had imported, the luxurious celebrations.

It takes the time to smoke a cigarette for the Ceauşescus to be condemned to the firing squad. The defense objects that this must be legal, this must be justifiable later. The prosecutor points out that they have ten days to appeal, and then in the same breath says that the sentence is to be carried out immediately.

What?

The camera is increasingly unsteady; the man holding it shakes from terror and excitement. The prosecutor points out, I have been one of those who, as a lawyer, would have liked to oppose the death sentence because it is inhuman. But today we are not talking about *humans*.

When it is time to bind the hands of the condemned, the dictator's wife screams and curses. Her voice overwhelms the tumult of lower male voices, making the sound band on the footage crackle. The mouth of a gun is pressed against her arm—they are pushed away, we see them crowded out the door by soldiers' backs. They are not blindfolded.

Suddenly the yellows switch to grays; everyone is outside on the concrete. There is smoke; it's difficult to see. Another hiccup in the film and there is the dictator's blurry wife collapsed on the ground, a dark rivulet of blood issued from her head. The dictator has fallen on his knees in a dusty heap. His body is turned over to show his face, to show the nation that yes, it is really him. Yes, he is dead. Sallow and bloated already.

The soldiers cover the bodies with blankets the same olive green as their overcoats. Then blackness.

But unlike the footage, the story will not shortchange you. You can see what the camera did not show, if you like. The story will tell you. You can make the image explode back into being, clean and crisp in the white winter light, without the fuzzy texture and off colors of something filmed:

The dictator and his wife clip-clop down the staircase, out into the courtyard through the double doors. The wife argues with the guards all the way to the wall, saying, This is wrong, you wayward soldiers will be punished. The men with guns are already there waiting for them, their eager weapons raised. This is when the Ceauşescus know they will die. Now. Not at some time in the future. One of the soldiers sees the knowledge pass over the dictator's face before he starts to cry. The soldier will never forget that look, that moment, the tears of the condemned.

The dictator starts to sing—what? The Internationale, of course. Nobody gives the soldiers the order to fire but they do anyway. They fire and fire and fire again, walking backward to avoid the ricochet, while the cameraman runs in, frantically fumbling a battery change.

No! he shouts.

But the bullets are already spent, the bodies already toppled. The wife does not die easily. She is racked by spasms, the back of her skull blown away. The only order given to the impatient execution squad is the order to stop. For a while they will mill around awkwardly, not looking into one another's eyes but not wanting to leave the place either. Their hands still thrumming with the metal click of the trigger, so sweet after such a long wait in the cold.

For years afterward the soldiers will meet up for drinks. The soldier who saw the look pass over the dictator's face will say, I had never even killed a chicken before. Eventually the soldiers will stop meeting up because they will always wind up talking about the same thing.

The wife was felled midsentence. The dictator did not make it to the fourth verse, the verse about reason thundering in its crater, about the eruption of the end of the past, about wiping the slate clean. In the pallid slanting rays of a cold Christmas Day.

When she moved into Andrei's apartment at the end of the first year of her studies, Irina became obsessed with the idea of a gun. She'd told her parents that she'd gotten work at the university and would share a place with some girlfriends over the summer. She'd grown used to telling her parents only lies. She couldn't very well tell them what was on her mind. The gun. Andrei had to have one; it had to be in his apartment somewhere. The image of it would not leave her. The cool metal in the darkness of some drawer, biding its time, waiting to show what it could do. But even if it was there, it would mean nothing. Any law-abiding American could stash a firearm in every drawer in his house, if he wanted. The gun was not what made Andrei a criminal.

The weapon had to be in the office. Irina was not particularly forbidden from going into the office, but she seldom did. Andrei didn't spend much time in there either. It was mostly a place to keep things. There was a handsome cherrywood desk, and on top of that desk a much less handsome small metal cabinet. In the desk and the cabinet were the things that Andrei kept for business purposes. The cabinet locked with a small key, but he was rather careless with it, often leaving it right out on the desk like a tiny beacon for curious souls. Irina, for a long time, did not betray what might have been his trust.

If Irina had to guess where in the office, she would guess in the tiny cabinet. She could have waited until Andrei left her alone in his apartment, as he often did, to look inside. She was not expressly disallowed from looking in there, so why would she have to do so surreptitiously? She went to look in the early morning, while Andrei was still asleep. Why did she push the door to his office open gently with one finger, so that it would not make any noise? Why was the plush carpet particularly intense against the pads of her bare feet?

The key was on the desk, glinting in the morning light like a coin tossed to the bottom of a fountain. Irina picked it up and almost jumped at the serrated sound of its insertion into the lock. It turned smoothly. The hinges gave a small squeak. She saw right away that there was no gun. Instead there were a dozen hooks bolted into the back of the cabinet. On each hook hung a small key—all the keys, coincidentally, much resembling the one that Irina had just used. On each key was a tag. On each tag was a five-digit number. They looked to Irina like a series of zip codes. She had merely unlocked her way into another mystery. She sighed and closed the door, letting herself plop into the rich leather desk chair that Andrei hardly ever occupied. She opened one of the desk drawers.

There it was. On top of a pile of green folders. Irina laid a hesitant finger on it. It was cold. She'd seen so many on television, but never a live one. It was smaller than she had expected but, she found when she picked it up, heavier than she thought it would be. Was it loaded? Irina had a sudden urge to hold the thing up to her face and peer inside the barrel. She wanted to look inside that narrow black mouth, listen to root out if it could tell her anything. Were there bullets inside the drawer? She did not see anything that plausibly looked like a box of bullets, but she did notice that on each of the green folders was a tag with a five-digit number. That was interesting. She reached inside the drawer to look at one of the folders.

"Try pointing that thing at me. It might make you feel powerful," said Andrei's sleepy voice from the door frame.

Irina was so startled that she almost dropped the weapon. Her lover did not sound surprised to find her there. Nor did he seem upset.

"Go on," he said placidly. "It's quite a feeling. Holding death in your hand."

"Is it loaded?"

He gave a small laugh in response and came to her, offhandedly plucking the weapon from her grasp. He pointed it at her and, before she even had time to be frightened, pulled the trigger. She gasped at its dry click.

"No," Andrei said.

"I would not advise looking through my things. For your own personal peace of mind, you understand," he said flatly. Irina nodded that she understood.

Any sane woman would leave a man after he pointed a gun at her, even an unloaded one. But Irina knew that she wouldn't.

"You gave me a good start, standing there pale in the morning light like that," Andrei observed. "You looked like a strigoi."

"A strigoi?"

The word caught Irina's ear. Andrei never used Romanian words with her, so this one had to mean something interesting.

"A revenant," he answered. "You would say a vampire. The creature you took from us and made into your vampire, to be exact. A restless soul that has come back from the dead because it thinks it has been wronged. It returns to settle its scores."

Irina wanted to ask why a woman would come back from the dead to sit at his chair and fiddle with his gun, but she didn't trust herself to make it sound like a quip. There was always the danger with Andrei that a quip was not really a quip. Jokes became real and the real became jokes. It was best not to tangle with this transmutation now.

"So this strigoi," Irina said, "is basically a ghost, not a vampire."

"Yes—no. It does eat the blood of the living. It hates the living. It has two hearts. To kill a strigoi, you must cut out and burn at least one of its hearts. If a strigoi rises from the grave and goes undetected for seven years, he can leave his native land, go someplace where they speak a different language, and become human again. He can even have children. But his children will be strigoi. So you see, it is a bit like a vampire but not quite."

"That's strange, the thing about leaving the country to become human again."

Andrei smiled. "Does it make you wonder how many of us immigrants are really truly the dead?"

His face looked gentle and stricken at the same time, not at all like the face of a man who'd just pulled a trigger on his young lover. Did he mean to include her in the mass of revenant immigrants? Was she part of this *us*? She'd seen the gun now, the real live revolver. She could never unsee it, never unhear the detonation of a future shot, never unsmell the bright red blood of a potential wound. She should fear such a wound—but maybe, maybe blood was not such a bad price to pay to finally feel part of an *us*.

The men expected the two girls to be friends, to get each other out of the way when it was time to do business. Elena might have been brought in to be Irina's companion as much as Vasilii's; it was easier to send two girls out for shopping sprees than one. On one of the trips to the desert city, Andrei shooed them out of the hotel suite, telling Irina that Vasilii was of the opinion that his new wife dressed like a cheap whore, that Irina should get her new clothes. Irina had almost replied, "So I can dress her like what? An expensive whore?" She had clearly been spending too much time around Dragos.

Elena was perfectly passive when Irina showed her what clothes to get. Short but not too short. Cut close to the body but not skintight. An enviable object but not one for public consumption. Whenever Irina asked Elena if she liked what was held in front of her, she said yes. It was true that everything seemed to look good on her—which was, after all, to be expected. Were the designers not imagining a young, slender body just like hers to drape their creations over? Elena looked over the figure she cut in the fitting room mirror, slinkily wrapped in a knee-length black dress that Irina had informed her was a basic piece for any woman's wardrobe. An open V-neck and narrow straps emphasized her delicate collarbone and shoulders. It was a stark contrast to the crunchy ballerina costume she had worn to marry Vasilii. Here she looked like a real, plausible ballerina, dressed soberly but elegantly for an arts fund-raiser where she would be proudly displayed to wealthy patrons, expertly performing not a dance but a courtship. Yet Elena's eyes shone with an inscrutable fever.

"Are you enjoying yourself?" Irina asked gently, as if checking on the comfort of a suffering patient.

"Yes, yes."

Elena seemed to be in earnest. She must have been trying to believe that whatever this was, it was enjoyment.

"You look very pretty," Irina reassured her. "You should buy this one."

"Not a bad purchase," Elena said carefully, as if she was repeating words that she had heard somewhere.

"Yes, it's very nice."

"He will not send me back home and ask for his money from the agency. I am not—what do they call it? Defective merchandise. Arm candy," Elena said. "I am good arm candy."

Elena sure spoke a lot of English all of a sudden. She was making sure she fit the dress, rather than making sure the dress fit her. Irina laughed, seeing in her mind's eye a pink statue of a pretty woman, fashioned of glimmering hard candy, being pulled through a doorway to a posh party by a well-dressed man. An unwieldy object to be consumed. What kind of grit might adhere to a vulnerable, unwrapped delicacy like that? Yet she could not be put back into the initial protection of her slick, sealed plastic wrapper. It was too late; she'd been opened. Eat or discard.

"Where are you getting these words?" Irina asked.

Elena shrugged. "People. Television."

What a thing to learn an entire new language from context, from scraps gleaned from exchanges she had no part of. Irina knew she had once done it with English herself, even if she did not remember.

After buying the dress, the two girls flipped the tags on fine lingerie on a different floor in the gigantic department store. Elena shouldered the crinkly garment bag holding her new clothes and fingered the black lace on a garter belt. She read aloud the name of the designer on the satiny label. "Funny," she said, "to wear some strange man's name against your skin."

Irina thought of the hands that had stitched together the rich silk, hands that were not the designer's. A nameless laborer, somewhere, in whatever country was listed on the label after the words *MADE IN*.

"Do you mean funny as in strange?" Irina asked.

"No, I mean funny as in funny," Elena answered absently, pinching the plush cup of a padded bra.

In the fitting room, Irina showed Elena how to fasten the tiny buttons on the garter belt to the top of a stocking. "That's what Vasilii will like," Irina said, "for you to wear things like that underneath so he knows it's for him only. Not for any others."

The lingerie set that Elena liked best was a saturated crimson that contrasted beautifully against her milky skin, with layered lace frills over the rump and at the breast line. Irina flipped the price tag hanging from Elena's waist and saw that this was the most expensive set in the pile of discards she had just tried on.

"You have good taste," Irina said, with what might have been construed as a touch of irony.

But Elena was not ironic. Her flushed face and glimmering eyes registered something like sad wonder. "I have never worn something so beautiful for underneath," she said, laying her hand on the soft upper curve of her lifted breasts.

Fear, wonder, amusement—this girl seemed to toggle from one inappropriate emotion to the other on a simple shopping trip. The source of the maelstrom from which these feelings were flung flummoxed Irina. "You are inscrutable," she said to the girl's reflection, as pretty and suggestive as something that might be seen in a men's magazine.

Elena gave a real laugh at Irina's observation and waved her off. "Oh, no," she said. "You will see. I am really quite scrutable."

While the cashier was ringing up the underthings, Elena looked up at a flicker in the fluorescent light.

"No windows," she said. "Like in the casino."

"Yes," Irina answered. "They don't want you to see time pass."

"This light," Elena said dreamily as Irina signed the credit card receipt, "this light is not a real light like the sun. But it is not darkness either. This light—this light is an unlight."

Unlight. Scrutable. This girl was full of words that were not words. In her mouth, English hardly recognized itself.

The first time was difficult. She was nervous. He could feel it in her limbs. The waves of tremor that traveled down her body as he kissed her were too strong to be caused by pleasure alone. He hiked up her shirt and nibbled her belly. She arched her back and gasped. “Do you want to?” he asked.

She dropped her head back onto the pillow and sighed. “I want to,” she whispered at the ceiling. “I want to.”

He slipped her shirt over her head to uncover the breasts that he knew were not encased in a bra from the way they moved. They were so young and so pert, absolutely lovely handfuls that he kissed with great reverence. She let him unbutton her jeans and work her out of them, and then her socks, which he grasped at the toes and pulled off swiftly, both at the same time. She laughed. It was a bit like undressing a child. She *was* a child! She was wearing the sort of white cotton panties that come in a three-pack from one of those American stores where they sell everything. He would have to get her better underthings than that, teach her how to dress properly. He relished the smooth sound of her skin as he removed the panties from her, and felt great tenderness at her expectant nakedness. She looked as desirous as any woman he'd ever seen, but also frankly afraid.

"Don't worry," he said. "I won't hurt you."

She said nothing but let her legs fall open slightly wider, so he took off the last of his clothes and positioned himself above her. When he nudged his way inside, it was his turn to gasp, while she gave a cry of pain that also happened to be quite arousing.

"You are one snug little scabbard," he said.

She was so tight it felt as if he were gashing the passage open himself. As if she were some fairy-tale nymph that he had summoned in order to split her into a woman, right then, with the insistent heat of him. He breathed to steady himself. He hovered there, halfway in. "Do you want me to go on?" he asked. Her glimmering eyes said yes.

He drove himself in. Her back arched and her body shuddered and fat tears began rolling down her red face. He paused again and was about to ask her if it hurt too much when she bucked her hips to urge him on. He made love to her smothering her cries with his kisses while she hung on to the strength in his upper arms with both hands as if she were afraid she might fall. After, he held her as a few stray tears dried on her cheeks. He expected blood on the sheets from taking such a stubborn, dense virginity, but there was none. Only a slight metallic tang on his tongue when he kissed her slit for being so good to him.

And she, not only despite the pain but also perhaps because of it, had finally discovered why she was born a girl. She would never forget what she had almost answered when he said he wouldn't hurt her. She almost answered, from some recessed place she didn't know was inside her, "You can hurt me if you want."

It was probably something he already knew; it was probably part of what had made him pick her out of all the girls in the world.

Opt

Once upon a time something happened. Had it not happened, it would not be told. Far away, there dwelt a king and a queen who, to keep their only son at home with them, were always making him fine promises they never fulfilled. Among these promises was the hand of the young princess from the neighboring kingdom. One day, the prince grew tired of waiting, and decided to set off in search of her himself. He called for his horse and his retainers and rode away from the castle. Why had he not done this before? Truly there was nothing finer than this open prairie alive with delicate yellow flowers swaying in the sunny breeze. Nothing finer than this new freedom.

The prince came upon a large rose tree with outstretched branches by a silvery stream. He dismounted to stretch himself. As he cupped the glinting water from the brook in his hands to quench his thirst, he heard a small voice sing out from the tree,

Beloved rose tree, open for me,
Let me cool my face in the pure brook
that bathes your roots
And pluck your sweet blooms to deck my brow.

The rose tree unfolded and its center parted to reveal a golden-haired maiden so beautiful that the prince was dazzled as if by the sun. She stepped out from the tree's dark gash to wash her delicate feet in the bracing flow of the cold stream. When the prince had recovered his speech, he approached her and said, Lovely maiden, if you will give me a flower from your girdle, I will give you rooms in my palace.

Impressed by the frankness of his manner and his ornate clothes, the maiden assented, giving him a tight white bud that augured an intoxicating fragrance in its full bloom. The prince asked for a kiss, promising that he would have her rose tree transplanted to his palace garden. When she gave him her darling pink mouth, he asked for the rest of her, swearing that he would make her a princess. Like most young maidens, the girl believed his flattery and gave him all that he asked for and desired. After, they fell asleep, entwined.

The prince woke before the girl, mounted his horse, and went on his way with his followers, leaving only a bunch of flowers in the lap of his sleeping conquest. Journeying on, he arrived at a golden palace studded with topazes. He asked the first man he met whether there dwelt a young princess in the palace. Yes, said the man, here dwells the Princess Lexandra, and I am the king, her father. The king was glad to extend an invitation to the prince with the view of his soliciting the hand of his daughter, for he'd heard of the prince's great wealth.

For some days, there was great merrymaking and pageantry in the palace. The prince found the princess as lovely as she was good, and willing to receive his attentions. His future father-in-law was pleased by the proceedings. The three of them set off in a chariot for the prince's kingdom, to present Lexandra to his expectant parents.

When the girl woke alone with a bunch of flowers as her only companions, she sighed and said, Dear little flowers, why did you make me sleep so long? Why is my beloved gone?

She stood up and went to the rose tree, singing out,

Beloved rose tree, open for me,
Enfold me and keep me safe
From the cold rising wind.

But the tree would not unfold itself. It shrank away from her with a hiss, answering only, Go away, undone girl, for you have sinned and can no more enter here.

The girl wept and screamed and kicked away chunks of bark from the trunk, but was met with only a hermetic silence. She thought of drowning herself in the stream. Instead she set off on the same road the prince had taken. After some distance, she came across a monk. She talked him into exchanging his rough frock and cowl for her fine robes. The girl went on her way, bundled in her new coarse brown garments. At the edge of a forest, she was sitting under a sprawling elm, taking a rest, when she saw a magnificent chariot drawn by eight white horses fast approaching. As it drew near, she recognized her faithless lover.

Good morning, young monk, the prince hailed.

Thank you, your highness.

Whence come you?

From the valley, your highness.

And what did you see there?

Nothing very extraordinary. A pretty girl weeping at the foot of a rose tree. When I asked her what pained her, she told me her story.

Repeat it to us, said the prince, attempting to hide his disquiet.

She said her home had been inside the tree, where she was loved and nurtured. Venturing out one day, she met a young man who begged for a flower from her waist, which she gave him.

The monk grew quiet, but the prince bade him to continue the story, which he did with reluctance: Then he asked for the flower of her kiss, which she granted—then the flower of her body, which she gave him also. He made many grand promises, but when the girl awoke from a long sleep, she found that the lad had deserted her. The tree would no longer admit her inside itself, saying she had sinned. For this, the young girl was weeping alone in misery.

Is that all? asked the prince.

As far as I know, for I left her crying there in the field.

To what town are you going, my young monk?

The same as your highness.

Jump into our carriage, then, said the prince, opening the door and making a place for the monk. During the whole of their journey, the prince queried for more news of the maiden, but could get nothing further out of the monk.

* * *

Arrived at the capital, the prince invited the monk to stay in the palace for the royal wedding celebration. The prince neglected the feasting, singing, and dancing in the great rooms of the palace in order to visit the monk in his chamber and speak of the rose maiden. He could not forget her, and stayed mute when the princess Lexandra asked him what was making him so melancholy and dreamy-eyed. The night before the wedding, the prince stopped off as usual at the monk's door, but when he knocked, he was answered by only a heartrending sigh. Breaking down the door, he found the poor monk swaying from the rafters, having fashioned a noose from the sheets on his bed. The prince rushed to cut him down. When the body fell heavily into his arms, he seemed to recognize its shape. He tore away at the rough cowl, and the girl's golden hair came tumbling out. He screamed when he saw her pale face, empty now of all its former bloom. He called his parents, the king and queen, crying, This is my princess! Do what you will with the other!

So the princess Lexandra was sent home with her father, with enough riches for a handsome dowry should some other prince happen along.

In the early morning hours between asleep and awake, Irina had flashes of what might have been memory from the time before memory, back in Romania. But these images might have also just been stories she'd been told. Or simply dreams from nowhere. The further she attempted to recess into the past, the more it was impossible to distinguish something that might have happened from something she might have been told. The further she went back, the more memory and myth were the same thing.

In the story her parents had told Irina of her adoption, her father was less enthusiastic about bringing a strange foreign child into the house than her mother was. He was a bit unsure, looking through all the portfolios of orphans. Then there she was, looking up at him from the grimy floor of some harrowing institution. The photo was in black and white so that he could see that the child's hair was dark and wavy but could not tell what color her eyes were. What struck him was how serious and intelligent she looked for such a young slip of a thing, like an adult soul trapped in a child body.

"What's her name?" he'd asked, without being able to help himself.

Her mother wasn't sure about it; she'd wanted a younger one, a baby. Irina might be more difficult. She already had a native language. She'd remember things. God knows what she might remember from that awful place. Low, narrow spaces. Running from a grasping hand. A closet. Footsteps outside the door. Waiting for the door to open, eyes wide open into pitch black, expecting the shock of light, but there was only the sound of the lock being turned from the outside. How long was she crouching among brooms and buckets in total darkness before someone let the light back in? There was a terrible thirst. But it's quite possible she doesn't remember, she is only dreaming, her eyelids fluttering without opening in the gray light of dawn.

After coming to America, she remembers things for real. For instance, being in the backseat of her American mother's trembling little car, idling while picking up her father from his job in the city. It was drizzling. She must have been eight years old. The rhythmic sound of the windshield wipers was interrupted by a definitive slam of the door, and then there was a smile for Irina as her father turned around to put his briefcase behind his seat. "Hi, honey, how was your day?" her mother asked.

Her father shrugged. "The usual." His suit was navy that day, pin-striped. Irina inhaled the slight scent of humid wool when he asked her, making eye contact with her through the rearview mirror, "And how was school today, Irina?"

She was about to say, "The usual," when her mother tapped her father on the side of the arm and pointed to a woman walking hurriedly across the street, shielding her hair from the light rain with a manila folder. She was pretty, though Irina could not tell you now what her face looked like—but she recognized female beauty in that brief flash of her. She had on high-heeled shoes and had a short quick stride limited by the snugness of her skirt, the vent in the back opening and closing with every step. Later in life, when she spent a lot of time buying clothes to please Andrei, Irina learned that what the woman had on was called a pencil skirt.

"Is that your new secretary?" her mother asked.

"Yes."

"What's her name again?"

"Hannah. Hannah Love."

When Irina's father uttered the secretary's name, her mother turned to look at him. "Really? That's really her last name?"

"Yes. Love, of all things," he answered wistfully, with a timid relish, even—while refusing to look at his wife. Irina did not understand the texture of the silence between them at the time, but it did make her pay attention. Her mother said nothing, and clicked on her turn signal to merge back into traffic.

When Irina told Andrei this memory, she also told him that later that year, her mother had wanted to adopt another child. With enough passive resistance her father eventually dislodged this idea. Andrei made a dismissive gesture with his hand. "Well, yes," he said, "a mistress will do that."

Irina had not meant to draw an explicit connection between the two memories, and felt a cold shock at the speed of Andrei's conclusion. "I didn't say the secretary was his mistress," she said, gathering the sheet to cover her naked body.

"One body for another," he said placidly. "That is the way it works. There might have been a mistress before you too."

How did Andrei do this? This relentless disdain for people, this ability to carve them up until all that was good in them was gone. How did he have this talent for making the world ugly when he was so handsome himself, sitting naked there in the tangled bed, all golden skin and lithe musculature and iron-gray eyes? He stripped and peeled and sliced everything until loneliness bled out of every cut, and Irina could not help but watch.

"Andrei," she said, "you're disgusting."

He gave a small laugh then, as if she'd told a clever joke. He was impossible to offend, as if he knew everything there was to know about himself and did not mind even the muddiest parts. "What is the point of pretending that most people are not empty in the middle? I embrace my emptiness—that is how fucking honest I am," he said.

The intensity of his gaze made Irina's sheet feel useless, as if he were looking right through it. Was that why she was with Andrei? His honesty?

"And you?" he said. "It must be you have no desire to be a good girl, else you would not be neglecting the shiny future promised by your postcard-pretty university to degrade yourself with me."

"Sometimes that future feels like a mistake, like I've been given all that I have by mistake."

It was not a feeling she'd told anyone about before, but she realized as soon as the words came out of her mouth that it was true, that it was something that had been following her around as long as she could remember, like her own shadow.

"If they'd left you in the orphanage, I can tell you what would have become of you," Andrei said. "There are many such children. You would have taken everything they gave you at that place until one day you couldn't. Say, maybe when you grew some sweet little breast buds, one day they would have added a good rape to your usual beating. That day something would have broken open in you and you would have said, Fuck this. You would have run away. You would have had nowhere to go. So you would have found your way to a metro station in Bucharest. You would have slept there on the floor on pieces of cardboard with other dirty children with no place to go. Sometimes you would have all been rounded up and had your heads shaved by the charitable organizations. To rid you of lice, you see. They would have given you clothes that you would have worn to tatters until they gave you some other clothes. But even with all the grime and the baggy sweater and the short, greasy hair, you would have been too pretty to pretend you were a boy. It's that plush mouth of yours, you see; it gives you away."

Irina looked at Andrei's face then, to see if there was mockery there. She could see none. He wasn't telling this story to torture her. He was doing something else.

There was a silence. Then Irina nodded. She wanted him to go on.

"It's hard being a girl on the street. Sometimes all being pretty gets you in life is more rape. You would have done the same thing all these children do to forget. You would have huffed paint from a plastic bag to dissolve your brain. You would have been one of the little ghost faces begging for pocket change at the hot mouth of the underground. With just a few coins, you would have had to choose between eating something and getting high."

"By now I would be dead," Irina said calmly.

"Maybe. Or you would have been rescued by nuns who would have taken you to a shelter to learn a trade so you could work in a factory—who knows. Or you would be a street whore with only two teeth in your head. It wouldn't matter. You would be one of those people who just don't matter."

The cruelty in Andrei was a hummingbird. It never stopped; it had to spend all its waking time feeding or it would die. It was a fast but vulnerable meanness that Irina wanted to touch to feel its small, frenetic pulse. It was as if she had to use Andrei, the way he treated her, to work her way back down to where she really belonged, down to the darkness that could swallow her and turn her into itself without her having to do a thing. All she had to do was not fight. Darkness was easy that way.

2

When she got this job, it took a little while to get used to all the money. But now Irina can stand in the vault at eight in the morning, gummy-eyed and cotton-souled, completely indifferent to the fact that she is holding a hundred thousand dollars in each hand. The hundred-dollar bills, bundled with yellow paper straps into tidy packets each worth ten thousand dollars, are cellophaned into large bricks, each worth a hundred thousand. The first time she held so much heavy, live money in her hands, she felt the possibility of escape detonate inside her like a tiny explosive charge: what if she ran like hell?

Now that she is used to cash in shipments from the Federal Reserve, she knows the money has as little life in it as crates of apples, or drums of cat litter, or bundles of newspapers. Cash is a dead tradable like any other. It was partly the double custody that made the novelty wear off so fast: every task requiring the handling of large amounts of cash must be performed by two people. This is a theft-prevention precaution. It also normalizes the operation. When Irina saw how thoroughly unimpressed the upper was counting all this money, it made her unimpressed too.

The upper today is Amy, one of the banking officers. The upper can also be the manager or assistant manager. The lower is always one of the tellers. Today it's Irina. The vault is opened with two combinations, upper and lower. Nobody knows both. There are also upper and lower keyholes for most locks. All the bankers have jangling bunches of keys, like prison guards or custodial staff. Some of them carry the keys as big lumps in their pockets. Some of them keep the keys attached to rubbery straps they loop around their wrists or their belts. Losing keys does not happen. Misplacing them for so much as a few seconds causes flares of hot panic that spread out concentrically through the bankers like waves from where a rock is dropped into a pond.

Irina keeps her keys on a large metal ring with a little claw she hooks onto her belt loop. Amy is one of the wrist strap people. In idle moments, she has been seen passing one finger through the strap and twirling the keys around in an offhand manner that makes the manager give her a disapproving look. Amy is not white but a honeyed shade of brown of ambiguous ethnicity. Her Anglo name offers no clarification, and Irina doesn't ask for any. She watches Amy feed packets of cash into the money counter.

"It always smells like feet in here," Irina says.

Amy shows the palm of one of her hands when she explains, "It's all the bacteria from people's hands festering in the paper."

It takes Irina a few seconds to realize that by "paper," Amy means all the piles of cash; she means the money is imprinted with more than ink. Ground into it is the sweat from countless unseen hands. Circulation has a certain organic stench.

Amy unbundles some hundreds and places them in the little top tray. She pushes a button; there is a leafy whir. They watch the machine pass the bundle and display the expected "100."

"So," Amy asks, "have you ever been in love?"

"What?"

Irina looks her coworker in the face, unsure of what is happening.

"Have you ever been in love?" she repeats.

Is Amy joking? Of all the words to say in a goddamn vault, "love" must be one of the most misplaced. Irina sees nothing but earnestness in Amy's face, which is in itself a trifle unusual. So she answers, simply, "Yes."

Irina sighs. She thinks she's given enough of an answer, but Amy isn't moving, isn't taking the cash back out of the counter to rebundle it. She plainly expects more clarification, and asks for it. "How was it?"

"It was a fucking disaster," Irina says.

Amy considers this answer and then shrugs. "Sounds about right," she says as she reaches for more of the money.

Irina does not yet know that this is normal. Being hermetically sealed in the vault alone with another person can do that. Maybe it's the confinement, all the sounds of the outside world totally blocked off by the layers of metal and concrete. Something about the vault will make a banker tell another banker about the abortion she's never spoken of with anyone before; it will make a banker ask another banker—a near stranger—what fears keep him up at night. Some weird thing about being inside the vault will suffocate the bankers with yearning to give voice to the inappropriate. Maybe it has to do with the presence of all the money. Cash in such amounts does things to the human mind that are hard to understand.

The house Irina is drawn to is just a few blocks from the tiny apartment she has inhabited only slightly, like a ghost, for the past half year. Every day when she passes the house on the way home from the bank, she knows it's time to pull the string and work her way to the front of the bus. Today, when she gets off the hissing bus into a breezy evening, she backtracks and stands on the sidewalk considering the house for several seconds. It's painted white with blue trim and has been empty since she moved to the neighborhood. The front door is ever so slightly ajar; in the end it's an invitation she can't resist. She nudges it open with a finger, thrilling at the idea that inside she might find some drug-addled squatter dozing on a bare, stained mattress. Or at least a raccoon looking at her wide-eyed from its bandit mask. But of course there is no one, just the lazy coil of dust in the slanting afternoon sun in the snug entryway. The living room, completely empty. Past that, a kitchen with a cheap Formica floor etched in mock tile, peeling up at the corners. The refrigerator door is left yawning open. On its shelving sits a jar of what must have been mayonnaise, the contents having turned a sickish shade of green. Why leave this? Were they in a hurry?

Irina searches for the evidence of illicit activities on this neutral site, however small the crime. Like maybe dead vermin. A mouse, the head wrenched at a sickening angle, the delicate pink feet curled inward and splattered red by the spilled innards left there when the cat had grown bored. Instead there is only a cobweb in the corner, glimmering in the light streaming from the picture window. There isn't even an occupant in the web, not even one bitty drained insect husk from a ghoulish spider meal. The room is actually fairly pleasant. The house simply won't cooperate with Irina's desire to make it a crime scene. She's watched too many cop dramas over her microwave dinners. Last night's episode was a touch more gruesome than usual: when the trench-coated detective found the body splashed all over the ground as if it had been dropped there from an airplane, he serenely pronounced, "Whoever did this guy in must have really hated his guts."

What an idea, that. Not only to hate someone, but even the meaningless tissue where he brews his shit. Standing with her hands in her jacket pockets looking out at a backyard bare except for a few scraggly weeds, Irina says aloud, "I hate his guts."

Does she? Her face feels warm. She lets the heat wash over her—whose guts? Oh, there is only one *he*, isn't there? As long as Irina lives she will never be rid of him. Without his touch her body is a hollow thing slowly dissolving, like a shipwreck soundlessly evanescing into the blind deep.

After working at a bank for a while, Irina can look down the line and guess who's overdrawn, the person she'll have to turn away without money. The broke are always so fidgety. And respectfully awed. To a person with a comfortable balance, Irina is a human ATM. To the poor, she is an oracle who tells them what kind of week they'll be having. If they have eight dollars, she gives them the eight dollars. If they have negative eight dollars, they will have to scrape up eight dollars for the privilege of having nothing.

Zero is a precarious number. It never lasts long. If they are lucky, a paycheck comes in. If they are not, the bank charges them for not having a balance. When Irina tells them they're less than broke, they generally take that news with the bleary-eyed resignation of people who are seldom told good things. Today a scruffy man tries to cash a check that isn't his at her window. He probably hasn't stolen it. Probably he's just found it on the pavement, freshly fallen out of someone's wallet, still folded in on itself like a daisy before sunrise. He must have thought, Why not? He has no plan, no fake ID. He just stands there like an empty vessel while Irina tells the assistant manager, who then calls the police. He mills around in the lobby waiting for them to come get him. He doesn't sit down since he knows the armchairs people sit in while they open accounts are clearly not for him. Why do the police even bother putting handcuffs on him? They probably could lead him away by the hand like a child who's cried himself exhausted. Jail is, after all, a place to go.

When he is gone, Irina rips a piece of blank receipt tape out of her dispenser. She looks at it for a full minute, at the serrated edge created by the perfect row of steely teeth. There are watermark stagecoaches on the paper, the bank's corporate icon from its picturesque beginnings as a shipping company in the old west. She picks up a ballpoint pen and scrawls, *Love, of all things.*

It is her father's voice she hears when she writes. Why her father's voice, when she was thinking of Andrei? She would rather not consider this question. She slides the receipt among her blank slips, green for deposit and red for withdrawal. It disappears there like a whisper in white noise, blending seamlessly with all the other paper.

"What was that you were writing?"

Irina starts. She didn't realize that Amy had been watching her.

"Just—ah—a message," Irina stammers.

"A message to who?"

Irina shrugs.

"Seems to me if you have a message, you should send it out, not tuck it away."

Irina caps her pen and opens her mouth to answer but finds it impossible to argue against Amy's simple, right logic.

The safe-deposit boxes line the entire corridor back to the inner vault. To access your box, you must sign a register and show identification. Then you are buzzed behind the counter and led down the metal hallway by a teller. You find your box amid an entire wall full of them. You put your key in. The teller puts her key into the second lock and turns both keys at once. The little door swings open without a sound; it's well oiled. You pull the metal box out of the wall, cradle it in your arms. The teller guides you to a stall where you lock yourself in and do whatever secret things you do with your box in there. Take out an emerald the size of a cat's eye. Put in some deed to a new property. Count flawless, investment-quality diamonds in a little velvet pouch pulled from the bottom of the box, under all the other priceless gems you keep in there. Look over documents certifying, after extensive genetic testing, that you are the true heir of the Romanov dynasty, and fantasize about the revolution that will put you back in power.

This is what Irina thinks you might be doing in there, as she mills around outside the stall waiting for you to come out with your mysterious box closed again, ready to slide it back into the wall. But today, while she waits, she is not listening to the shuffle of your unseen papers. She is not thinking of you or your box. There is another box. She follows the numbers along the wall to find it. Here it is: 21012. It is one of the big ones along the bottom. When someone pulls one of those out of the wall, it is sometimes heavy enough that Irina has to help the customer carry it into the stall. A blank innocuous little metal door among thousands of blank innocuous little metal doors, snug between 21011 and 21013. If Irina opened it, would it give her the explanation she is looking for? What explanation is she looking for, anyway?

They haven't come for her. Fine. But how is it possible that they haven't come for the contents of this box?

She can hear you closing your lid. You will be out soon. Certainly, if you knew what she is thinking, you would tell her to stop running her finger along the smooth edge of the little metal door while smiling sadly to herself. Be reasonable, you would say. That box is not rightfully hers to open. It doesn't belong to her. It would be better for her to throw away the key.

It's not so much that she is suffering terribly; it's that she is waiting. Waiting in the same way that an elderly patient on a morphine drip waits in his hospital bed: too much pain, time to go. Waiting for it to come get her, the queasy suspicion growing that it will not, that she is the one who is supposed to let go and surrender to her own death.

Of course they won't come. All this waiting around is stupid. It's pure masochism. She should throw that damn key away and forget the whole thing, or she should open the box and take whatever is inside. Instead, she indulges her slow decay.

After Andrei sent her away, she started to lose her hair. She did not even notice until the day the barrette she used to clip it into a ponytail every morning slipped right off because there was no longer enough hair to hold it there. The jarring, tinny sound of it hitting the tile—only then did she truly see the serpentine black strands circling the drain in the shower all this time. All those mornings she had glanced over them without understanding what was happening. She is not in her body. When Andrei withdrew, he must have taken her away with him.

Will her hair come back? Will she?

Irina doesn't believe her identification papers when they say she is young. And yet when she looks in the mirror, she sees a smooth jaw, an unlined eye. Her face does not match the leaden weight of the sluggish blood stagnating in her veins.

Before she met Andrei, she suffered from a peculiar kind of female amnesia. She would come home from class bone tired. So weary, in fact, that her eyes were closing of their own accord before she could get through dinner. She would make her way to bed in underwater slow motion, sometimes falling asleep still fully clothed. The sleep was a hood pulled over her mind. When she woke up soaked in clammy sweat, she could not remember what nightmare had shocked her eyes open in the darkness.

This would happen for two, sometimes three nights in a row. She'd puzzle over herself, wondering if she was getting sick, and then in the morning her breasts would be hot, sore, heavy. Some small punishing monster roiled in the pit of her belly. It paced its tender chamber and tore down the wallpaper. When it was furious enough, it flung furnishings out the door: blood.

It was only that, blood. This whole woman thing again. How could she forget this every month?

But when she was with Andrei she never forgot her femaleness. He trapped her in this vulnerable state where she could be penetrated. Even now, she cannot forget. It comes upon her at unexpected moments, a yearning so sharp it slices through the core of her, her body's insistence that it was made soft to make him hard. A disturbance, a sudden volcanic eruption into a quiet ocean—here she is all red molten rock, all black plumes of ash, all hissing heat boiling away the tentative equilibrium of life that had just begun to bloom again. Here she is polluting herself.

There was something about the other girl's body but Irina could not tell what. It was as if Elena contained some kernel of knowledge that offered glimpses of itself while refusing to give a full reveal. As clear as a mirror image, and somehow as untouchable. Irina watched her do slow, leisurely laps in Andrei's small blue swimming pool, wondering how she could move through the water without her tiny string bikini exploding off her. Irina was also wearing a bikini, a sturdier one with ruching in flattering places, splashed with a pattern of large flowers. It was reminiscent of something a pinup might wear. Had Irina put on red lipstick, curled her hair, and sat in a coy pose, she might have been a painted woman winking down from the nose of a World War II bomber.

Elena's bathing suit was plain red. It was unclear whether there would have been room to fit a pattern on the bitty triangles of cloth that barely made her outfit legal to wear publicly. She looked more like something out of modern Hollywood than Irina did. Irina admired the lithe lines of her body as she rose from the pool and came to lie down on a chaise longue without patting herself dry. Everything was pert and trim. Her hip bones jutted out slightly from her flat stomach. Her rib cage, her clavicle—so many bones exposed. They made Irina feel heavy.

"What?" Elena asked.

"You are very pretty," Irina explained.

Elena looked down at herself as if to check on what Irina had just said. "You are prettier," she answered. "I look like a child. You look like a real woman."

"You could be a model," Irina said.

Elena shook her head as if she had already tried that tack. "Not tall enough," she said. She indicated a pair of fuller breasts on top of her own. "I want your breasts," she said.

"Yours are adorable," Irina answered. "They'll never sag. Mine would fall out of that little top you're wearing!"

"Can I take it off here? I want to tan."

Irina didn't see why not. There was no one else out here with them. The landscaped apartment complex was so quiet under the dazzling sun that it felt empty of people. Besides, if it was against the rules to strip down, who would come set them straight? The police? The homeowners' association? Elena reached around her back and pulled the string to undo the knot. She slipped off the halter without untying it and let it drop to the ground without looking at it. Beads of water glinted on her skin. Her rosy nipples drew Irina's gaze.

"You too," Elena said, motioning at Irina's top. "You do not want lines in your tan, no?"

Irina was about to say no. She had always been the kind of girl who hugged her breasts to herself while changing in the locker room so that others would not see. Clearly, Elena would have been one of those girls who walked to the showers buck naked, talking loudly with her friends, proud of her pride itself. Or not—what did Irina know of her, anyway? What did Irina even know of herself? In a matter of months, she had turned from an innocuous model student to a willing accessory in God knows what. She had been a gifted American teenager, and now she was what? A gun moll? It wasn't precisely rebellion that had pushed her here. It was a kind of curiosity, maybe the same spirit of query that made an addict try one harder drug after the other. There was no good place to go down this path. But down was the most fascinating direction.

Irina's heart beat fast as her top plopped wetly on the concrete next to Elena's. For a couple of quiet minutes, the two girls roasted silently in the sun.

"You fluster!" Elena said with a giggle. "I can feel you fluster at your nakedness. You are such an American."

"What if a man saw us out of his window?"

"Then he should pay us." Elena laughed. "Men pay to see young naked girls, don't you know?"

Irina breathed deeply, making a conscious effort to relax.

"You should not be ashamed," Elena said. "They are very nice."

Irina was unsure how to respond to that. Her customary response to compliments was a simple thank-you, but this seemed wrong under the circumstances. The second default response was to give another compliment in exchange for the first. Somehow this felt less inappropriate.

"I like your haircut," Irina said.

"Ah. Yes. I had long hair, like yours. Longer than yours.

Down to my ass, like a princess in a fairy tale. I had the hair when I sent Vasilii my photo. Then one day I was tired of all the weight. Had it all cut off. My mother cried. I showed her I got money for it, but she cried anyway. Said it was so beautiful. She did not want any part of the money. I would have felt bad but I was so light, so light without it. No big heavy weight down my back. No catching it places, or sitting on it. Instead of the hair there was just air. Just freedom. When they sent me to Vasilii, I was told maybe it had been a mistake, to cut off the hair. Maybe he had chosen me for it. They sent me anyway. The first thing Vasilii said when I got off the plane was, 'You cut off your hair.' I said, 'Is that bad?' He said, 'No. But you need new clothes.'"

"You have lots now."

"Yes. What he meant was I needed more clothes. More clothes on my back. More covered up. He said I smelled of cigarettes, and a woman should not smoke."

"But Vasilii smokes!"

"Vasilii is not a woman. Sometimes when he is not home, I steal one of his. But I try not to. I do not want to smell of it. But it is hard. I am hungry all the time. But I try not to eat. If I become fat he might send me back. He said he did not care about the hair, but he does not like his women fat."

It was strange, to hear of Vasilii and women. He'd seemed so unconcerned with them before the night he'd explained the appeal of young girls to his business associates.

"You don't miss your hair at all? Sometimes I think of cutting mine, but I'm afraid I'd miss it."

"I do not miss the weight. But it's true, the hair, it gives you something to do. Maybe I would not have cut it if I knew how much time I would have here, how little I would have to do!"

Elena laughed then, and shook her short curls. "Come here," she said. "Sit. Let me braid you."

Irina sat at the foot of the chaise longue, Elena close behind. She closed her eyes when she felt Elena's slender fingers stroke her scalp.

"Your hair," Elena said. "Warm from the sun."

"Because it's black."

"Naked women braiding each other. This is like the banya."

"The banya?"

"The public bath, in Moscow."

Irina pictured steam, many naked bodies. Not young and pert like the two of them, but of all sizes and ages. Scars, rolls of fat, moles, jiggling, gales of laughter. The forgetting of men. What did a fat old woman look like naked, really? Irina did not know. Those were not the kinds of nudes that were shown in magazines and at the movies. Elena had seen women in the flesh, many of them. In unflattering light. Unretouched. Not posed to sell something. Irina wanted to ask if they were very ugly, if they were scary to look at. If looking into her own young body's unsightly future made her shudder. But no. Maybe, Irina thought as she opened her eyes to look up at the cloudless blue sky, maybe there was a strange kind of comfort in it.

Not too far from the big casinos, there was a bar owned by a man Andrei did business with on his many trips to the desert city. In the bar's basement were three rooms: a small one with a table and chairs, for meetings; a larger one with shelves, for storage; a larger one still with a stage and seating, for a show. The show that was put on there was not advertised anywhere. Still, on performance nights it drew a decent-size audience composed of men who bought tickets with their drinks at the bar. When Irina and Elena arrived at eleven thirty, it was still early enough for downstairs to be empty. They could sit on any of the plush red velvet seats with cup holders that the bar's owner had purchased for a steal from a shut-down movie theater.

"Get all the drinks you want," the owner said to the two girls.

"How long will you be?" Irina asked Andrei.

"Until Vasilii comes back," he called as he disappeared into the back with Dragos.

"The show starts at midnight," the owner said as he closed the door behind the three of them. "Enjoy, girls."

The inflection in his voice made Irina order a plain cola from the bar. She wanted to stay lucid for whatever was coming in case she had to think quickly. Elena had a fruity mixed drink, an icy alcoholic slurry layered in shades of pink and red with both a cherry and a little paper umbrella on top. The stage was shielded by a curtain that matched the velvet on the seats. The room was bathed in quiet music and dim, aquarium lighting.

"What kind of show?" Elena asked Irina.

"Dancing girls, I'm guessing."

"Well, I know *that* much, but what *kind* of dancing girls?"

At a quarter to midnight, the two television screens bracketing the stage flickered to life and started playing a cartoon. The cartoon looked old. Snow White was wearing a dress with a yellow skirt reminiscent of the one worn by her Disney self, but this was clearly a different version. In this version, she lay on her back on a table with her skirt hiked up while the seven dwarves, being dispensed to her on a conveyor belt, mounted her for a few hasty thrusts and then rolled off. There was something ancient and primitive about the whole repeated display, like a relief of a fertility rite chiseled onto a tomb wall. Snow White's wicked stepmother watched the whole scene in her magic mirror while pleasuring herself with a lit candle. Whenever her body engulfed the tiny flame, she breathed fire out of her gaping mouth.

"Well, this is weird," Irina whispered into Elena's ear.

"Probably German," Elena said with a smirk.

By the time the cartoon was over, a couple of lone men had come in and sat behind the two girls. When Elena went to get more drinks, Irina could feel the men's eyes on the back of her neck. She made the mistake of turning around. One of them raised his wineglass to her and smiled. It seemed a long time before Elena returned with another sweet boozy confection for herself and a plain glass of seltzer for Irina.

At midnight, the light grew dimmer, the music grew louder, and the curtain parted. A woman in a sparkly Arabian Nights getup shimmied onto the stage. In slow, smooth movements, she divested herself of her entire outfit, even her bejeweled thong. Though the woman was naked save for the gold lamé stilettos that made the muscles on her calves stand out like tense ropes, Irina felt a vague sense of relief wash over her. This wasn't so bad. It was even a bit campy, like cross-dressing. The dancer's false eyelashes, her completely hairless body, her costume made her hardly more real than the strange German cartoons. When the music stopped, she picked up her clothes, giving the audience a wink and a wave when the curtain closed on her. The television screens displayed more cartoons in the interlude before the next act.

Bubblegum pop by a teenage starlet blared over the speakers when the curtain rose on two blondes in schoolgirl outfits with tartan miniskirts, white shirts tied above their bellies. These schoolgirls wore black patent leather stilettos and black shadow on their heavy-lidded eyes. They circled each other as they removed their costumes, starting with the tiny backpacks that jostled against their taut rumps. Their pigtails swayed with their gyrations. Once they were completely naked, they kissed. Irina looked around. There were more men in the audience now, including a rowdy cluster that had come in together and was occupying the entire back row.

Then the two dancers sprung glittery, baby-blue dildos from their tiny backpacks and began shoving them inside each other.

A high, lone whistle came from the back of the room. Elsewhere a man laughed. Irina took a careful sip from her chalky-tasting seltzer. When the song ended, the performers exited the stage with all their gathered props, shiny dildos bobbing jauntily in their clutches. The cartoons started up again. Elena giggled. Irina felt her warm, sweet breath against her neck when she whispered in her ear, "What would happen if we kissed like the two girls in the show right now?"

"They are already watching us," Irina replied, the edginess in her voice making Elena look around. The two of them stuck out in the audience so that even the men who were thoroughly absorbed by the show snuck glances at them when the cartoons came back on. The place had filled up. The two girls were surrounded by alert male bodies. The air was warmer and the music louder. Irina breathed easier when only one woman came out for the next act. She danced deftly using a chair. Her flexibility was impressive. Then something unexpected happened: a man appeared onstage. He paced leisurely around the dancer, offhandedly flinging dollar bills at her at regular intervals. Each time she was showered with money, the dancer removed an item of her clothing. When she was naked, the man stopped. Everyone was paying attention. The whole place was electric with anticipation.

"Will they really fuck?" Elena asked Irina with a sly look. Irina wondered at that moment if there was more inside Elena than alcohol. She was about to ask whether Vasilii or Dragos had given her a pill when the man onstage exploded out of his tear-away clothes. He took the dancer by the hair, roughly bent her over the chair, and shoved his professional-size erection into her waxed slit. He thrust in time to the throbbing music.

Irina was fascinated by their unchanged facial expressions. This impersonal piston action didn't seem possible to her—how was this sex?

The performers continued their blank mating in various acrobatic positions designed to give the audience the best views of the entry. Irina could not take her eyes from the woman's face. Her lips were parted, but her eyes remained as distant as those of a factory worker performing a rote task. How could she have something that size pounded into her and not make a sound? Maybe that was why the music was so loud—to cover up any sounds. Irina thought maybe she saw the woman wince.

"That girl," Elena said.

"What?" Irina could barely hear her over the blasting music.

"That girl," Elena shouted over the thrumming bass. "That girl up there is Russian like me."

"How do you know that?"

"Her face. She has a Russian face."

How far had the dancer traveled in her lifetime? Was this possibly the least degrading job she had ever held?

The song seemed to go on exceedingly long. Possibly, it was being played on a loop. Finally, it ended, and when it did, the man and the woman simply disengaged and waved good-bye to the restless audience as the curtain disappeared them from view. After that there were other pairs in various costumes. Irina would not be able to remember later how many or what they were wearing or what the wafer-thin premise of their storylines were. The displays of dominance by the men became more aggressive as the night wore on. One man spit into the woman before he penetrated her. One man whipped a woman before taking her by the neck. Elena did not seem in the least alarmed, so Irina decided she should not be alarmed either.

It was past two in the morning when Irina noticed a tattoo of a leaping dolphin on the lower abdomen of the absurdly endowed man onstage. What a strange thing. A dolphin was a hopeful symbol you expected to see inked on the ankle of a sweet-faced college girl—or, if she was daring, on her lower back, peeking out above the waistband of her low-rise jeans. But right above the drugged cock of a pornographic actor? Irina looked up at his face. He must have felt her eyes on his, for he looked right back at her while giving his mate an offhand smack on the ass. It was horrifying, but Irina would not look down. She would not look down. The song was winding to its noisy crescendo. Had he just winked at her? She could not be certain. What was certain was that he pulled out of the orange-skinned bleached blonde he was sodomizing, pulled her head roughly to him, and came in her mouth. At the sight of the semen dripping down the woman's chin, the entire pack of men surrounding the two girls was palpably galvanized. A large hand squeezed Irina's thigh. She stood up abruptly, shaking off the unseen grab, and shouted in Elena's ear, "We're getting out of here. Now."

It was at this moment that Vasilii entered the basement, scanning the darkness for the door to the little meeting room. Irina had never been so happy to see him. She pulled his limp wife to her feet in order to bring her to him, stumbling over men's knees and feet to reach the one man in the room she was hoping would offer safety.

* * *

"How was the show?" Andrei asked Irina on the limousine ride back to the hotel. It was a casual question that could not have been asked with a casual intent.

"There were cartoons," she said carefully. "All perversions of fairy tales."

"Yes, that's right," Andrei said. "Dragos thought those were very funny."

Dragos laughed and said, "Those monster cocks are going to give our poor girls nightmares."

Irina wasn't sure whether he meant the cartoon or flesh-and-blood ones. Andrei had known what the show was, yet still he had left the two girls to watch it alone. Why had Andrei wanted her to see such a thing?

"They never took their shoes off!" Elena observed with a strange, awry glee, before leaning into her husband's shoulder and closing her eyes.

"Those girls," Andrei said pleasantly, "they're poor girls thrown away by their families. But they're lucky enough to be pretty, so an agency picks them up and tells them there's work for them. A job in America is a plum job for girls like that."

The place had been a showroom, of course. The performers were displaying their skills onstage to later sell them privately to willing men in the audience. Irina thought of their slender ankles wobbling in their high, high heels as they milled around the audience after their turn onstage, waiting for offers. Her womb cramped up suddenly and viciously.

"Those girls are lucky orphans," Andrei said, turning his head to look out the window at the passing lights of the desert city.

That was what he meant. Irina was these girls and they were

her. He was offering her alternate selves. It was a sick kind of gift.

Irina cupped the pain in her belly with her hand. There was something she ought to say to Andrei, to all three of the men, but she could not tell what. She looked at Elena. Elena was draped limply across Vasilii's lap, asleep. Or at least pretending to be asleep. It would have been a clever move, pretending to be asleep at a moment like this. The sort of willful checking out of a bad situation an agency girl would learn. Closing the eyes and leaving the body behind for whatever was in store for it, while the mind was elsewhere, not having to know things it would rather not know. Elena was from an agency too, like the dancers.

Irina was Elena and she was her. They were all lucky, lucky orphans.

Cars. Irina knew that the business meeting in the building she was waiting for Andrei to come out of was about cars. She'd heard that much when he was on the phone that morning. Rows and rows of glinting cars in a warehouse somewhere. A warehouse Vasilii owned that Irina had never seen. She imagined standing in the middle of it among all the empty, silent carapaces of shiny cars receding infinitely into the darkness. The warehouse in Irina's mind had no walls, only luxury cars parked so tightly together that not a single one could be driven anywhere.

Thousands of cars disappeared every year off the streets, but the cars in Vasilii's warehouse were not those cars. The stolen cars were broken down into parts. The parts were shuffled and put back together as different cars. These reconstituted cars were given new coats of glimmering paint before making their way to Vasilii's warehouse. From Vasilii's warehouse, the cars would be loaded onto container ships to be sold overseas. It was a good, fast business. A business so good, in fact, that Andrei could have meetings about it in conference rooms downtown, in the same spaces as men who did their business in the open, legal world.

There was something about the cars that Irina liked: you could take things apart and use the parts to build new things. Being pulled into the underworld was not so much the end as another beginning. That was the way people thought of weddings—as new beginnings, Irina mused as she gazed at the dress in the glass case. The dress was not quite white. It had a cream bodice, and a full skirt in the faint golden color that retailers call *champagne*.

"Want to try it on?"

Andrei startled her. Irina hadn't heard him come up behind her.

"How did it go?" Irina ignored Andrei's question.

Andrei shrugged. "You know. Investors can be fussy. But it was fine. Everything's moving. So you want to try that costume on or not?"

"Don't be mean, Andrei."

"Why should I be mean? I want to see how you look," he said as he guided her into the bridal shop.

The sales representative eyeballed them suspiciously the moment they walked in, and she raised her eyebrows when Andrei asked her to let Irina try on the dress in the window. "Do you have an appointment?"

"Why should I need an appointment? There is nobody here."

The representative was already bristling in her tidy suit as she slowly looked Irina up and down. "Are you…a relative?" she asked Andrei.

"I am her dear uncle. I think that dress there will quite dazzle the whole family when they come from the old country for the wedding, no?"

"Do have a seat, then," she said, designating a lavender velvet divan. "I will take her to a fitting room."

"If you will allow, I must go with her to put her in the dress. It is traditional, in my country, you see."

Was he stilting his English more than usual? Hamming up his accent? His request gave the saleswoman pause. She was clearly evaluating him, evaluating the two of them. The cut of Andrei's suit meant that he could clearly afford the dress, so she let him follow. She parted heavy white curtains and ushered them into a brightly lit room lined with large mirrors, with a small round platform at the center for the bride. The saleswoman watched Irina hesitate, afraid to step up to it.

"Do fetch us the frock," Andrei ordered. "I will undress her."

She didn't answer as she let the curtains fall shut behind her. Andrei laughed. "Did you see that look she gave me? She is dying to know what barbarous country I come from where it is customary for uncles to dress and undress child brides! You can do anything if you say it is the custom in your country. Americans are so afraid to offend."

As he offered his hand to guide Irina to the platform, he added, "Americans of a certain class, anyway." He stood back to look at her and then sat on a plush chair in the corner of the room. Everywhere she looked was another nervous reflection of her—and somehow only one Andrei, taking them all in.

"Undress for your uncle," he said, and her heart hiccuped. She slipped off her sandals, wiggled out of her jeans, and pulled off her T-shirt. It was alarming, in a way, how fast she was standing there in the expensive underthings that Andrei had bought for her. The distance between clothed and unclothed was so short. The sales representative came back as Irina was draping her things on the chair next to Andrei's. In the representative's arms, the bagged dress looked as voluminous as a body. "It's lucky," she said, "our bride is just the sample size." She was about to sidle into the fitting room when Andrei stood up and took the bag from her. "You may go, thank you."

"It's kind of complicated. There's a petticoat—"

"Yes, yes, I am quite familiar with such things, thank you." Andrei gently pushed her away, and at this point the representative flashed Irina a look that said, *There is something highly irregular here; this is not how these proceedings are supposed to go.* After he had gotten rid of her, Andrei laid down the big crinkly bag and unzipped it. He rooted around until he found the petticoat, an enormously full, ankle-length skirt boosted with tulle.

"Are you really quite familiar with such things?" Irina asked, amused.

"No, but how much of a science is it, really? See, you just open this thing here and step into it and pull it up and close it again. Get back on the podium."

Once fastened on, the petticoat was a little snug. Even through the protective slip, Irina could feel the crunchy tulle against her legs. "It's itchy," she said, "and it looks lumpy."

"Well, it just needs to be arranged a bit." Andrei knelt at her feet and began to uncrinkle the crushed tulle until it was fully fluffed. It was strange to see him there, tending to her clothes like a mother. When he was done, the petticoat felt enormous, a halo of white swallowing her lower body.

"I look like a meringue," she said.

"Well, that's what brides are supposed to be, no? All sweetness and air," he answered as he pulled the long champagne skirt from the garment bag. "Raise your arms now."

Irina submitted and closed her eyes as she felt the cool fabric slide over her face. She opened them again when she felt Andrei tug the waistband to fasten it. The yards of golden satin felt heavier than expected. The platform had almost entirely disappeared beneath the prodigious outfit, the train unfurled to take up almost half of the room.

"What lovely pageantry," Andrei said, sighing. "Now for the top. You will have to take off your bra, darling; otherwise the straps will show."

Why did Irina blush? Had he not seen her breasts many times before? And yet she felt more naked than ever, her skin electric with anticipation when he fitted the bodice over her torso. It was a corset with a sweetheart neckline, an ivory satin jacquard with a leaf pattern and a golden border at the top to match the skirt. Andrei gave the laces a good yank, cutting Irina's breath as the severe paneling pressed in on her body. "Oh, I like that gasp," he whispered, as if the sly glance he gave her in the mirror when he tightened the corset further wasn't enough to let her know that he wanted to fuck her now. He wanted to fuck her right there in the fitting room, hike up all the crinkly white fluff under the long skirt and fuck her while she braced herself on the cold mirror with the flats of her hands.

"You're dreadful," Irina said. "She'll hear us."

"It would be better if she fetched us a veil. I wonder if she would fetch us a veil. Do you feel like a virgin?"

"The dress isn't white."

"You need to reach in and hike up your tits, dear niece, so

they bulge nicely out the top."

Irina did as he asked, her breasts cool and heavy in her heated palms. "I should buy the dress and marry you," Andrei said. "Give you a proper Romanian family name."

The girl in the mirror was Irina but not quite. With a complicated ceremonial white dress, a girl could be pieced into a bride just the same way a new car could be pieced together from several old ones. The dress had power. Irina looked like a painting she'd once seen in a history book. Another pretty woman in a big white dress, the consort of a Romanian head of state. It occurred to her for the first time that the painted woman, under all the white fluff, had a body.

"You won't buy the dress, Andrei, so you better not stain it with come," Irina said with a sarcasm she hoped would steel her.

Andrei snorted derisively, smiling as he tied up the laces. He didn't have to say that it didn't matter if he stained the dress with come. He had enough money to buy it even if just to throw it away. He didn't have to point out that whatever Irina said, her body was ready for him, that she wanted him to fuck her, that she always wanted him to fuck her, it didn't matter if the corset was stiff enough to hurt her, tight enough to make her dizzy—she always disastrously abjectly pitifully wanted him to fuck her.

"If you faint," he said, breathing in her ear, "I will cut you loose."

Şapte

The colors of the image are saturated, almost touchable. The orange velvet on a posh armchair matches that of the curtains in the background, heavily tasseled. The tablecloth is a vivid blue. The bright red of a sash across the subject's chest signals his rank, along with the golden sheen of his clustered military medals and the braiding on his collar and sleeves. A ceremonial sword is at his side. It is not known whether the hues are a touch darkened because this was the painter's style, or whether the lighting in the room where Alexandru Ioan Cuza sat for the portrait was a little dim, or whether the darkness is the accumulated grime of passing time on the paint. Still, plainly visible here is the face of a man long dead. A handsome one, it seems, with well-defined cheekbones, a well-proportioned nose, and a neatly trimmed beard, his gaze looking not directly out at you from the painting but slightly to the right of you, so you are compelled to glance over your shoulder to catch what he sees there.

Perhaps he is a touch melancholy. Or just bored: it is long

and tedious to sit for a portrait, especially when there is so much to be done. When the principalities of Wallachia and Moldavia were allowed to elect their own heads of state by the Ottoman Porte, they both chose Cuza, handing him the task of stitching together the idea of this new nation, Romania. Handing him the task of breaking the choke hold of the boyar class on the peasantry—the boyar class into which he was born. He is noble as they come, though he cannot trace his bloodline to any of the true voivodes. His long and illustrious heritage may be fit for a king, but he is not a king, and perhaps that is part of his downfall. The new nation, in the pained and dazzled moments of its fledging consciousness, needs a man of flawless lineage, a man with a number or a superlative for his last name, a man they can call voivode.

At four o'clock on the morning of February 22, 1866, they break into the palace. They make him sign his abdication. This happens because he tries to do too much too fast; there is a conservative backlash. It happens because there is an ugly scandal with a mistress. It happens because history says so. On the following day they are kind enough to escort him safely across the frontier. They will import a king from Germany who does not speak the language of the nation he is to rule, but he will try his best.

Cuza settles in France, the modern country he had attempted to mold the new Romania after, with his wife and his two illegitimate sons by his mistress and his mistress herself, who bears the same name as his wife who bears the same name as the scandalous mistress of the one they will call the playboy king who bears the same name as the wife he left her for, the mother of the next king, who bears the same name as one of the daughters of this next king who will be the last man Romania will ever call voivode, who bears the same name as the wife of the dictator who will be executed on the day of the birth of our Lord in the year 1989. There are so many dead Elenas, it is hard to keep them straight.

The homonym, Cuza's wife, you may look at her portrait too, if you like. This one is unfinished, a sketch for a later official portrait. Ink, pencil, and a dash of dilute watercolor to give texture to the dress—but no real hues. You can see the brushstrokes on the yellowed paper, which is in some places turning brown. In its voluminous stateliness, the dress is in its way as impressive as her husband's military vestments. White, a color that shows the slightest speck of soil immediately. Yards and yards of satin with many bows, with much delicate lace at the neckline framing her bare shoulders. There are untold petticoats under her dress, untold boning in her corset to form the large, beautiful bell shape that blooms forth from her tiny cinched waist. A rich, inverted, many-petaled flower. The dress must be heavy, trapping heat with frightening efficiency in its many layers. There is skill in moving gracefully in such a contraption, in not making it look like the enormous impediment that it is. Like her husband, she rests one lax hand on a table. His fingers trail on documents that must be of importance to the welfare of the state. Her fingers arch gently over something that looks like a small box, closed. Some feminine object we are not to identify.

She looks more determined than her husband, perhaps being more used to stillness and boredom, but her gaze, like his, does not fix you directly. Her eyes look slightly to your left, so that once again you are compelled to look—over your other shoulder this time. Still nothing. Was she wearing such a prodigious dress when they burst in on her husband as he was spending the night with his mistress, to make him sign that odious paper? No, probably she was in her nightclothes. Still white, but gauzy and free-flowing. She did not understand what was happening when they sequestered her in her apartments, did not know that she would be gone the next day and would never set foot in the palace again when she shielded her startled eyes against the light of their torches.

At least the overthrown would be allowed to keep their sons, their two sons. The sons of Cuza born of one Elena and raised by the other, born of the mistress and raised by the wife who would not have to watch them die for many more years. A coup d'état, they called this sort of seizure then. Two centuries later they would call it a putsch, when the last man that Romania will ever call voivode would be toppled by a dictator. The dictator is dead now as you look at the painted face of a consort of a bygone head of state. The last king, the last man Romania has ever called voivode, he is alive and in exile on this very day. This very day on which you can visit a replica of the big white dress Cuza's wife wore in her portrait, in a museum situated in the palace built by the imported German king, home of the current Romanian president.

There was a game the boys used to play with the girls after school. Rather, it was a game the boys inflicted on the girls. It was quite simple. The boys gave the girls chase; the girls had to run. Sometimes the girls would get away. Most of the time not. When a boy caught a girl, he would tackle her and pin her down on the ground. He'd straddle her, pinioning her arms to her side. He'd lean into her, practically nose to nose, and give her a choice: kiss or kill? If she chose kiss, it was usually a quick peck on the cheek, and then both children would turn red, laugh, and run away. But sometimes one of the older boys went for a bolder kiss, a lingering one on the mouth or neck. There was less giggling then, and fiercer blushing. Such occurrences were only occasional, and usually secret. It was considered in bad taste to tell someone about a kiss, which didn't keep many stories from getting around anyway.

If the girl chose kill, the boy was free to give her a punch. A certain gentlemanlike code dictated that it be a light one on the shoulder or upper arm. If a boy put his balled fist into a girl's stomach or face, he would be shamed. But when this happened, the girl seldom told, because some of the shame clung to her also. This didn't necessarily make any sense, but then nobody was quite sure exactly what the point of the game was, or even how to win. Yet the children kept playing. Oftentimes a boy would chase the same girl he always chased. Oftentimes a girl would be offended if no one gave her chase. It was all a great muddle of feelings, a harbinger of puberty, like swift-moving clouds darkening the sky before a downpour.

There was one boy who always chased Irina. She was a hard one to catch. If he managed to get her, by the time he had her pinned, his breath was ragged and fast. He could hardly get the question out: kiss or kill? Invariably, Irina chose kill, looking him right in the eye. This would fluster him. Turning his face away, he would deliver a weak open-hand slap to her left shoulder, just below the clavicle. Then the two children would get up, dust themselves off, pick up their schoolbags, and go their separate ways without a word. Irina was quite sure she hated this boy. She hated his upturned nose and his chapped lips. She hated that he relentlessly picked her. Even more, she hated that little sissy whack he gave her. She remembered another girl who had grown irritated with the persistent attentions of a particular boy during this game. One afternoon, when he went to give her chase, she did not run. Instead she jumped on him and gave him a good wallop. He left her alone after that.

The boy who chased Irina was not bigger than she. Certainly, if she fought back, she could solve the problem of his affection. Why did she not? A pacifist streak. An unshakable respect for the rules of the game. A part of her that liked the boy after all, maybe. No. Rather, it was a perverse sort of politeness. It was better to endure these little enactments than to be rude.

Then one day something happened inside the boy. It must have been that he was just about out of breath, he was just about to lose her around a corner. But this time he could not let her go. He reached out with his hand, unsure even of what he was lunging at, and caught a fistful of her streaming black hair. His fingers closed around it; she stopped short and yelped. Before either of them knew what was happening, she was down and he was on top of her.

"Are you crazy?" she said, completely devoid of her usual calm. Her scalp stung.

"Kiss or kill?" the boy demanded, as if she'd said nothing.

The two children stared furiously at each other. Irina was feeling a great roiling something that she did not understand, and it occurred to her that she was feeling this something because he was feeling it, that she lay beneath him, helpless, reflecting him like a mirror.

"Kiss, then, if that's what you want!" she hissed, her eyes slitted like a cornered cat's.

The boy looked down at her, at the rich, long tresses he'd just yanked fanned out around her face on the pavement, and suddenly he was at a loss. Irina was rather beautiful like this, and rather frightening. He wanted to put his hand on her face to feel the high color of her cheeks, the blood pumping beneath her skin. Had he ever been so uncomfortable in his life?

He raised his hand, slapped her in the face, and ran away. He never again gave her chase. The prospect of her yielding again terrified him.

To this day, even now that he is a man, the boy remembers

this episode with startling clarity. When he thinks of it, it makes him smile at the vagaries of children, and yet it still embarrasses him more than it should. Irina, now that she is a woman, remembers the feel of a boy's hand grabbing her by the hair and pulling her back in some chasing game after school. She remembers the raw pain and shock of that moment. But she does not remember what came after. She does not remember that his hurting her made her yield. She does not remember the sound or feel of his slap. Now that she is a woman, she never thinks of that boy anyway. She wouldn't be able to summon the image of the upturned nose or the chapped lips that she used to hate so much. She doesn't even remember his name.

She loved the lingerie, the details on the diaphanous fabric. The seams on the stockings; the little buttons, covered by a tab of silk ribbon, with which she fastened the stockings to the garter belt; the lace edging on the panties; the tiny red rosette at the joining of the molded bra cups. The slow removal of all these things, like a ceremony. She loved the contrast between the pageantry of the female costume and the way that wearing it—being divested of it—revealed what she came to feel was her truest self. At least her happiest self: the female unwound, exposed, blessedly unthinking. As if the performance called up the real. As if it was the presence of the lace itself that left her unsheathed and tremulous and fully realized in the arms of the man who had summoned her. As if he were a sorcerer and she his nymph. If she thought about it in her calmer moments, the process was actually a bit terrifying. To be made woman, one who could be penetrated. She had a feeling that he could wound her deeply and irredeemably in such a state, yet she could not help but yearn for it.

He'd say to her, "Be soft for me," his accent almost completely melted from his whisper. She'd answer, "So soft you won't know where I end and where you begin," as if she were answering an incantation, a prayer. He was so different when he made love, so present and devoid of irony. Perhaps those moments were what made her stay. But no, she needed him in all his guises. His cruelty was as necessary to her as his love. He awoke in her a nakedness so complete it could not possibly end well.

Andrei is not back yet?" Dragos said without so much as a hello first.

Irina opened the door only slightly wider when she saw who it was. "Not yet. He shouldn't be long."

She was supposed to invite him in, sit him down and offer him a drink while he waited. She was supposed to let him step out of the heat into the air-conditioned cool of the entryway and lead him to the plush couches in the living room. His white shirt had the top two buttons undone and looked wilted on his body, the sleeves rolled up to the elbows, exposing the dark down on his forearms that crept onto the backs of his hands. He wore a small gold pendant, plainly visible in his open collar. Irina made out for the first time that it was a Saint Christopher medal.

"Good luck for travelers," she said a little stupidly. He took her observation as an invitation to come in. When he did, she shut the door behind him, automatically turning the lock. A definite click.

"Do you always do that?" he asked.

"What?"

"Lock the door when you're here. Lock yourself in."

"Yes."

He went past her and sat heavily on the black leather sofa. He made himself at home, tucking one of the yellow velvet pillows behind his back to give himself support. He looked up at Irina standing there.

"Drink?" she said.

"Andrei would not have some țuică, would he?"

"No."

"No, he is not nostalgic for the homeland, that one. Vodka, then. With ice."

When she handed him the drink, the cold dew on the glass made it slip from her loose grip. Dragos caught it quickly; the ice rattled. There was not a drop spilled. Irina thought she felt the brief heat of his hand against hers. There was something electric in the contact, a tiny jolt.

"You only brought one," he said. "You are not drinking with me?"

Irina shook her head.

"Pity."

He took a generous gulp from the glass, wincing slightly when he set it down. Irina was about to sit on the love seat cornering the couch when Dragos said, tapping the cushion next to him with the flat of his hand, "Now now, Irina, sit with me."

She complied automatically. When their knees touched, he did not move away. Irina was about to readjust so they were no longer in contact but something curious in her decided not to. Something in her wanted to know how long he'd sit there like that with this tiny touch between them, through the rough linen of his pants. How long before he'd move away? How long before he'd acknowledge it?

His dark eyes were on her, making her feel the slightness of her short, light summer dress. She was highly conscious of what the fluid blue silk did and did not cover.

"That is a new dress, no?" he asked.

"Yes."

"It's true, you do not have much else to do, besides buy new dresses."

She pulled her leg away from the warmth of him, settling back into the couch. "There's university," she said.

"Yes, that. It is history, is it not, that you are neglecting to study?"

"Yes."

He didn't stop looking her over, doing so with deliberate slowness, as if he were trying to gauge exactly how all her parts fit together. He was a bit stocky but not bad-looking. There was a nervy quality to his body that made him radiate energy, enhanced by the potential harm in his flat, black gaze. He looked like a man who had a gun hidden somewhere on his person. Women generally liked this about him.

"So, you are getting along well with Vasilii's little wife?"

"She's interesting. I like her."

"How much English does she speak?"

"More than you'd think."

"Now I am the only one without my own little woman," Dragos quipped. "I am feeling a bit lonely—"

"Dragos." Irina interrupted him.

"Yes?"

She hadn't known where she was going, saying his name like that. She'd said it in a warning tone as if attempting to veer away from a dangerous place, but it hadn't worked. There they were. It was a strange feeling, this stark awareness of every inch of her bare skin, of the whisper feel of her dress against her breasts, the small of her back. Usually she understood clothes only in terms of Andrei. She only put on clothes for Andrei to take off. When she picked out a new outfit in a store, she inevitably thought of his golden-brown hands divesting her of it. But now here was another man who looked as if he were trying to imprint himself into her clothes.

"Did Andrei tell you?" Dragos asked, a slight smile playing on his lips.

"Tell me what," Irina asked dryly, without the rising inflection of a question.

"He is such a gentleman, sparing your delicate ears. He didn't tell you."

He took a sip of his drink while she waited for him to explain himself. She would not offer him the satisfaction of asking again. Dragos set the glass back down on the tabletop sonorously. "The other night I got a little drunk," he said. "You know. We were talking about women again. Vasilii would not tell us about his nuptial bliss—so private with his pleasures, that man. Andrei told me to stop bothering him, and I offered him ten thousand dollars to fuck you."

Irina inhaled sharply, as if someone had stuck a needle in her somewhere. She said nothing, a high flush slowly creeping up her face.

"I am sorry," Dragos said. "That is a bit low for a fine thing like yourself. You must understand, it is a low price between friends."

He did not sound at all sheepish. Was he putting her on? He had that in common with Andrei, the ability to make people unsure whether he was joking. He was even worse than Andrei that way.

"You don't want to know what he answered?"

"You're disgusting."

Dragos smiled broadly and then licked his lips. He stared absently at the entryway and said patiently, as one presenting an obvious argument to an intelligent audience, "My dear, I could teach you some first-rate tricks to take back to your man. It is clear to me you would make an excellent student."

He did not touch her, did not even turn his head to look at her. What if she slapped him? What would that feel like?

"I don't like. This joke. At all," she said quietly, trying to sound angry rather than scared.

There was the remnant of a smile playing on his lips. "Just let Andrei know, my dear, when it begins to matter if it is a joke. Then I am sure he will ask me if I meant to be funny."

The itch to hit his smug face was unlike anything Irina had felt before. But what if he liked that? He might be that type of man, who'd take any display of passion as an invitation. He was liable to hit her back, pin her down on the couch, and fuck her immediately, her flimsy silk dress hiked up past her ass. He wouldn't even bother to remove her panties, merely pull them aside before he shoved himself into her. She hated him so much.

The two of them were staring at each other with peculiar

rage when Andrei's key turned in the lock. It was almost a disappointment to have everything diffuse as if a timer on a bomb had abruptly been stopped. Irina wanted to see. What would have happened if she'd been left alone with Dragos for another minute?

When Irina and Elena returned to the hotel suite at the appointed time on the afternoon of the day after they had seen the basement sex show, the party's guests were gone. A black woman in a blue dress with a white apron was clearing away silver trays that still held a few stray canapés, glasses in which the ice was melting into remnants of vodka.

"Elena, let me teach you about America," Dragos quipped. "See? A genuine colored maid. One of the staples of this fine country."

Nobody laughed, and the woman went about her work as if she'd heard nothing. Vasilii made eye contact with his new wife, and she went to him immediately. He ushered her into his room with his hand on the small of her back, closing the door behind them silently. Dragos and Andrei gave each other a look, and wordlessly Andrei led Irina into his own room of the suite.

On the coverlet of the four-poster bed lay a small burgundy booklet and a plastic card. "These are for you," Andrei said, designating them formally with his hand as if they were priceless jewels. Irina picked up the booklet. It was emblazoned with gold lettering and an eagle bearing a sword and a mace, with a cross in its beak. The eagle had a coat of arms for an abdomen, and etched on this shield were two more eagles, what looked like a bull's head, a lion, a pair of some sort of fish. Dolphins. The lettering at the top read *UNIUNEA EUROPEANĂ*. At the bottom, *ROMANIA*, and then, slightly smaller, *PAŞAPORT*. Irina opened this unforeseen object to its first page and saw herself. A photo of herself. An accurate description of her height and eye color, but a falsified date of birth. A blank signature line. An unknown name.

"What is this? Who is this Vasilica Andreescu?" Irina asked.

"She is you, if you will have her."

This was definitely the most peculiar gift she had ever been given. It made a great cold suddenly pass over her.

"What—what is this person for?" she asked of the strange passport.

"She is a good place to keep some money. A place through which to pass money," Andrei explained. "And for this place we need a body."

"You are giving me a passport and a bank account for a girl who doesn't exist. So that you can launder money."

Andrei looked a little stung. "You don't like it?" he said plaintively.

This new identity would make her more than a girl who consorted with criminals. It would turn her into one of them. The problem was not that she didn't like it but that the prospect was rather attractive. The new name had the draw of a beautiful new dress. It had a pretty drape that gave her body an appealing shape. It promised that she might be seen in a new way by new eyes.

"You will seldom be asked to do anything or present your face anywhere," Andrei said soothingly.

Irina picked up the plastic card, a bank card. "How much is in there?"

"A respectable amount. But you must understand this money is not at your disposal. If you move it in a way that is not consistent with orders, bad things will happen."

Irina stopped breathing for several seconds. "You would hurt me?" she asked.

"No. I would not hurt you, darling. But I could not keep you from getting hurt."

Who had come up with this idea? Was Elena, in the other room, also being offered an alternate self? Irina flipped through the passport again. "It's a very good fake," she observed.

"That is because it's not a fake," Andrei noted. "We know people. This is a real passport. As far as Romania knows, Vasilica Andreescu exists."

So a nonexistent woman with Irina's face was a Romanian citizen. Here were her blue eyes, her pale skin, her curtain of wavy black hair. Here was her unsmiling, slightly puzzled expression. Irina couldn't even remember when this picture was taken. The perfectly blank grayish background did not give her a clue. Perhaps she could peel away the translucent film of her life and find beneath it the other's life, the life of this Vasilica Andreescu. Vasilica Andreescu, a world traveler. Well moneyed and of legal age. With a bank account like that, it was unlikely that she'd been thrown away by her family. She was not an orphan like Irina.

"I can't believe what you're asking," Irina said.

"Look, you can be a girl from the old country." Andrei's touch felt warm against her cold hand as he murmured into her ear, with something like tenderness. "You see, darling? A proper Romanian name."

She was about to laugh and ask when he had gotten so patriotic when Dragos walked into the room and set a big black briefcase on the bed, where they were sitting. The way the briefcase sank into the plush coverlet made it look enormously heavy. Irina instinctively reached to put her hand on the fine pebbling of the expensive leather. She almost decided to spring the case open at that moment to see what was inside. But what did it matter? She would not pollute herself with knowing what was in it.

"So, what does the lady say?" Dragos asked Andrei. "Does she agree with our request?"

The two men looked at Irina, who looked back at them without opening her mouth.

"The lady says nothing," Andrei replied.

"Good," Dragos said, "since everyone knows that when a woman says nothing, she means yes." He picked up the new passport and leafed through it, as if looking over a piece of furniture to check whether it was well built. "Ha!" he laughed. "Vasilica Andreescu, named after her two fathers. Very clever."

1

Irina cannot reach zero today. After closing time, she counts and recounts all the cash in her box but keeps coming out fifty dollars over. Balancing at the end of the day is usually a task that brings her a dull satisfaction: all those columns of numbers, which, in the end, add up to a perfect 0.00. No such luck today, just that accusatory +50.00. At least it's a round number. It is worse when she is off by some completely inexplicable number, like 13.56 or eight cents. With this tidy overage, she can fathom what must have happened. She knows that it is highly unlikely that she shorted any customer fifty dollars. That would have brought forth a howl of recrimination that she would have corrected immediately. It was probably a typing error when she was entering the amounts; perhaps she transposed a 3 for an 8 somewhere. A findable fault.

Usually when this happens, she is supposed to call over the manager. The manager counts all the cash once more. Then he and she, the unbalanced teller, go through all her transactions from the entire day, looking for the overage or shortage. Sometimes it can be found from this pass-through, and the mistaken record can be expunged and replaced with a correct one. Sometimes it cannot, and she must fill out an Out of Balance ticket that turns into a little black tick on her record.

But it's not so much the black tick that bothers Irina today; it's the time. She wants to go home. The prospect of sitting there flipping through papers and computer screenshots with her boss for another half an hour turns her exhaustion from the workday into a heavy weight in her body. There is another solution, of course, one that she has not yet seen fit to employ because she is trying to maintain the idea that she is a decent person. She could just take fifty dollars.

Of course doing such a thing would show up on Irina's monthly balance statement as shortage after central processing digests all her transactions and rights any errors. But that is just a sheet she will have to sign at the end of the month, maybe with a brief contraction of the brow and a grumbled comment from the manager. A tiny consequence. She would be accused of nothing. The sky would not tear open and thunder its judgment at her. Everything would proceed as before. That's one thing that she's learned happens after doing wrong: everything goes on just as before. You are not found out. There is a whole lot of nothing.

She would be fifty dollars in the red. But who cares? In the red is where she's lived her whole life.

Irina's fatigue is now crushing. The thought of time ticking away while the manager counts all the cash in her box, his thick body disconcertingly close to hers as he roots through her workstation—it's too much. She heaves a deep sigh.

She knows it won't do to simply take a fifty out and pocket

it. There would be security camera footage. She'll have to be smooth and discreet, but she knows how. She swiftly fingers one of the bills from the correct compartment as she fits the lid over the cashbox she's pulled out of her register, slips it into the pocket from which she takes out the keys with which she then locks the top of the box. She performs this with the same blank face she always wears while wrapping up her day—the absence feigned this time, as the theft makes Irina completely present in the moment. When one is doing wrong, everything takes on a fascinating resonance—the weight of the box, the clang of the enormous vault locks, even the placid face of the manager. Even his "See ya tomorrow" feels portentous. She is familiar with this high. She knows that when she gets home and unfurls the fifty from her burning pocket, Ulysses S. Grant will flash her the sly glance of an accomplice. She hates that she knows and likes this feeling. She hates how much she looks forward to taking the money out of her pocket and having a good look at what she has stolen.

These days, Irina counts a lot. She does it with such fast, machinelike exactitude that the management puts her on the merchant teller line. She takes large cash deposits from local businesses, having to count everything by hand. It is more intensive work than the regular customer line, and she does not get paid more. But it's nice. She gets to know the merchants. For instance, the man who runs the bird feed store around the block always flirts with her. Sometimes when the line is long, he squats with his cash bag while he waits for her, dreamily tilting his head and looking much like an inquisitive parrot on a perch. There's also the plump lady from the cake shop who feels compelled to mention her fatness in every conversation so she can deliver her most valuable gem of wisdom: Never trust a skinny pastry chef. Then there are the church people, who speak softly and bring in the most cash.

Today Irina is absolutely overwhelmed by the church people: so many deposit tickets, so much cash in small denominations that her register is glutted with it. She cannot close her lower drawer. The whole box is so heavy with money that it threatens to tip over. When Amy walks by her, Irina grabs her sleeve and whispers urgently, "I need to sell to the vault. Now."

"Holy shit! Look at that. How much do you have in there?"

"Probably fifty K."

"Oh fuck. Yeah, close your window right away. I'll get a ticket."

Irina puts out her *NEXT TELLER PLEASE* sign with a decisive *thunk* and quickly gathers forty K of the cash. She can't quite hold it all in her arms; on the way back to the vault Amy has to pick up a couple of bundles that fall onto the floor behind her. The *thwap* of cash on carpet makes several customers turn their heads. The two bankers hustle into the vault, shoving in the overflowing money.

"Jesus," Amy says as she begins feeding the bundles of cash through the counter. "How many fucking churches do these church people do the books for? Religion is an excellent racket."

"It was Easter last weekend."

"They must have passed around collection buckets because plates can't handle this kind of volume. Hey, guess what other business must take in that much cash in small denominations?"

"Tell me."

"Strip clubs!"

Irina cannot help but smile, and then asks if Amy has ever worked in a bank branch that had one in the neighborhood.

"Nope. I mean, I'm just saying. I mean, can you imagine getting all those dollars crammed in your G-string? You don't know where they've been."

"What about us? We have to handle those dollars."

"Gross. Shit—now I won't be able to count small bills without picturing them in some girl's ass crack."

Irina laughs at the idea that many of the bills that were just handed to her from church collection plates had also been slipped into a dancer's thong. The cash looks so innocent fluttering through the machine, just bits of paper that either like or do not like being handled. If the bills are new, printed fresh from the Federal Reserve, the packets are too tight and the bills stick together, spectacularly jamming the counter. They have to be painstakingly counted by hand. All the tellers fight against this inevitability. They take the money and crumple it violently in an attempt to roughen it. They smack the packets hard against the walls, trying to loosen the bills. The higher the denomination of the bills, the harder the tellers smack them, the more the tellers roughen them: it's more important for the big bills not to stick, for an extra one not to be given to a customer by accident. The new bills are so sharp and crisp that they cut the palms of the tellers' hands as they are counted. The tellers hate the new bills, even if they're cleaner. They like the soft old ones, more like cloth than paper. From a G-string or not, the old bills are better; they go through the automatic counter with a smooth uninterrupted whir.

"Amy," Irina says while bundling the cash, "have you ever been robbed?"

"No, but I used to work with this guy who was once. When the robbers came in waving guns, he was holding the night deposit bag. While they weren't looking at him, he dropped the bag in the garbage chute so they wouldn't get it. He was commended for saving the bank a bunch of money. I think they gave him football tickets or something."

"But—what if he'd been shot?"

"I know, right? What a chump. Like I'd risk my life for other people's money." Amy gathers some bundles, puts them away. "Okay, that's the ones. Give me the fives."

Irina pauses before she hands over the fives. "Did he say what it felt like to have a gun pointed at him?" she asks.

"Yeah," Amy answers. "He said it didn't feel real."

Irina almost says that it felt real enough to her, but then doesn't. It's a close one, and it scares her. She almost inadvertently talked about Andrei. He is still so near the surface. At that moment, she envies, of all people, Elena. Elena used to have long, thick, beautiful hair. Then one day she got tired of it, cut it all off, and never missed it. Irina used to have long hair too, but most of it fell out. She chose not to see until it looked so thin and bedraggled that she had to cut it short. She still misses all the hair she has lost. It's stupid of her, this yearning for things that are gone forever. She hates it but she can't help it.

These days, Irina counts a lot. She does it with such fast, machinelike exactitude that later in the day, shortly before closing time, a wary customer asks her to count the money again, but slower. Twenty. Forty. Sixty. Eighty. One hundred. She lays each hundred dollars in a fan of five twenties overlaying the previous fan of five twenties. Then she gathers up the money, taps it into a neat little stack to hand over. The customer hesitates before he takes the money, as if he is somehow suspicious of her. Irina smirks at his leery eyes.

She is thinking about a small key she has packed away in her things that she brought with her when she left Andrei. Should she carry the key on her? Should she work it onto the heavy ring where she keeps all her other bank keys? Would using this key push her back into the past or propel her into the future?

The key is so small and discreet, a tiny golden presence with the number faintly engraved on its handle: 21012. A palindrome.

Yes. She will carry the key on her. At least until she figures out whether opening the box the key is fitted for is a good idea or not. Whether it is a step backward or forward.

Sometimes buried things need to be dug up again to be put to rest forever.

Meanwhile, the man who just left Irina's teller window with a twice-counted bundle of twenties walks away with her message. Eventually, it may reach you. Eventually, he will spend the money.

This morning, Irina had written on one of the twenties she gave him, in a fast scrawl right across Andrew Jackson's face:

You never were.

Artificial lighting. The low white noise of quiet human voices discussing money and its movement. The flutter of paper. A sore lower back from standing all day. The muscle memory of a rote task endlessly performed with an absent mind: Greet customer; accept papers; perform transactions with automatic fingers dancing on the ten key, spilling numbers on the screen so fast that they look uncontrolled but are not; count cash if there is cash; tear receipt tape from machine with a deft flick of the wrist and hand it to the customer. "Thank you. Have a good day." The serration in the machine's dispensing slit makes perfect tiny teeth on the thin paper. Irina was told to say, when trained for her job at the bank, "Thank you. Have a nice day." For some reason, the word "nice" does not suit her, so she substitutes the word "good." It seems less simpering, more sincere—even with the customers for whom "Have a good day" means "Fuck you."

The greeting when picking up the phone is also scripted. It has a certain rhythm that always makes it come out in a singsong. But lately a growing spirit of mischief has made the syllables a touch malleable in Irina's mouth. Sometimes, when a supervisor is not within earshot, Irina says with all the cheer she's been instructed to put in her voice: "Thank for you calling Hell's Cargo. This is Irina speaking. How may I help you?" So far no ear has chosen to register her improvisation.

There is a lull in the influx of customers. Irina distractedly fingers the edge of the collar on her sober houndstooth blazer. She thinks of the stitches there. She thinks of the stitches everywhere, all over her, down to her underthings. The hands that put the stitches there. The unconscious memory written into the musculature of those hands, their rote tasks. The artificial lighting. The white noise, the loud continuous ticking of the sewing machines. The ticking lulled the hands into a kind of rhythmic trance. Sometimes only the exhaustion and the aching joints from the repetitive motions told the hands that they had been there working the entire day. Hours were swallowed. Time hovered, then skipped. Slowed, sped, then disappeared in crumbling chunks.

The woman with these hands liked that all the other hands in the factory belonged to women like her, even the boss. Men would not bother with her at her age. The hands had a handsome bone structure, but the flesh was worn past tautness. There were veins and lines, an emerging frailty. There was a safety in aging, in not being looked at anymore. Safety in being able to cast your eyes on anything you liked without it being interpreted as some kind of invitation by some man on the hunt.

The slightly rough cloth passed easily between the fingers on the nimble, practiced hands, the hands that had made this jacket so many times before that they could do so without input from the brain, or even the eyes. This jacket, the jacket Irina might have taken off the clearance rack in a windowless, big-box store. This might be the jacket that Irina had selected as looking suitably bankerly for her new nobody job in her new nowhere world. Where did the tag say it was made? She would have to take it off to check.

Then, one day, there was a man pacing the floor of the factory. The hands did not remember hearing that the woman who supervised their sewing would be leaving, yet there was a man now. Younger than the woman who owned the hands, but not too young. Wisps of thinning hair at his crown, perpetual half-moons of perspiration at his armpits. His close presence made the hands skip nervously, his breath hissing past the neck of the woman who owned the hands. He called the woman who owned the hands by her identification number, not by her name. He clearly knew her name; he was just playing with her. Her eyes looked up at his smug face, a great weariness creeping over the hands. How nice it would be if this man were not here.

He leaned over the workstation. She could smell him. He laid his finger on a crooked little blip in the stitching on the collar and said, "Unsatisfactory." Was it on purpose that he brushed up against the hands when he pointed out their faulty work? The woman who owned the hands wanted to say, *I would not have done that if you were not here*. It was possible that her eyes communicated these words anyway because the man looked offended. "This piece is not suitable to be sold," he said. "Its cost will come out of your salary."

When he was gone, the hands put the jacket aside to take home, since they'd bought it anyway.

Irina wonders if the callused hands had done delicate work, if they had put together small, diaphanous clothes meant to be looked at by only one man at a time. Did the woman who owned the hands ever think of the bodies their work would encircle? Did this woman ever suspect that the clothes she made might wend their way across the world to the infant girl she'd tried to forget so long ago? What a choice, to bring a child into this broken world and then give it away. Irina used to wonder what choice she would make under similar circumstances. Now she knows.

Irina pulls the top drawer open on her till. She peels a ten-dollar bill from the top of a stack of them. She chooses that denomination because, of all the dead white men on the currency, Hamilton in the most handsome. At least his representation is the best-looking of all the representations on American cash—who knows what the past really looked like?

Irina plucks a pen from the mess atop her workstation and writes, to the right of the oval portrait of the man who would never be president because he died in a duel before history tapped him for the job, in a loose forward-leaning scrawl: *a mother's hands*.

They told her that the procedure itself would likely not last more than fifteen minutes. They said she would be awake. She didn't want to be. She didn't want to see or feel anything. They told her they would put her in something called conscious sedation. A twilight state. Likely, she would not remember a thing. She hoped sincerely that this was true.

She had made the mistake of asking what they would do, how such things were usually done. They said she would lie on an examining table, just like for a routine pelvic exam. The walls of her vagina would be held open with a speculum, and then the cervix would have to be dilated. Then a tube called a cannula would be inserted. A suction machine would be activated in order to evacuate the uterine cavity.

When they said "evacuate the uterine cavity," she waved her hand for them to stop talking. But then she couldn't help herself. She had to ask, "Is it still alive when it comes out?"

"It depends on the patient."

"Is there a face?"

They did not answer this question right away. Before they could speak, she thought better of it and waved them off again. Better not know. Don't tell me. Just get on with it.

The first time they tried to slip the IV in, her hand was shaking too badly and the vein collapsed, blue and bursting. Blood saturated the medical tape. She looked with disbelief at the large bruise beginning to spread over the back of her hand. It would be there for weeks, turning all sorts of colors, from black to purple to a greenish yellow to blue—a garish display of angry blood vessels. At first, it would hurt worse than it looked, and after, it would look worse than it hurt. Then it would fade, leaving a barely visible white nick on the back of her hand.

Rather than try on the back of the other hand, they put the IV into the crook of her elbow. She looked away when the needle went in this time. At first it was only a saline solution; they would mix the sedative in with that. It felt strange: she could feel the veins near the puncture site outlined in cold until the fluid warmed up in her blood. She had never felt the shape of her veins before. For a moment, the novelty of the sensation distracted her, but then she thought of it again, a thing they had mentioned offhandedly but which burrowed terribly inside her brain. She remembered that two weeks later she would have to have a follow-up examination—this to make sure that she had not developed any complications, and that the procedure was complete.

"You mean sometimes the procedure is *not* complete?" she'd said, her fear sounding like anger.

"This very rarely happens, and is easily mended."

She did not care how easily mended it was. She could not shake the image of dead parts left inside her. Surely she would feel them, know they were there. Surely her dreams would be eaten by tiny ghosts. What if something came out? A bitty hand, still grasping for an invisible thing. Or worse, an unseeing eye.

"Irina," they said, "we will administer the anesthesia now. Try to relax, all right? Count backwards from ten."

"Zece," she said.

Her eyes shot open. She was convinced she would remember everything. Every scrape. She would not be able to speak and they would not be able to tell that her unblinking gaze was fully cognizant, that her mind was recording.

"Nouă," she said.

Why was she counting in Romanian?

"Opt," she said, turning her face away from the painful white of the light above.

Maybe this was the nightmare. Wake up, she told herself. Wake up.

"Şapte," she said.

There was a roar—she never made it to şase.

Şase

Once upon a time something happened. Had it not happened, it would not be told. There once was an emperor who ruled over a whole world, and in this world lived an old shepherd who had three daughters: Anna, Stana, and Laptiza. Anna, the oldest sister, was so beautiful that the sheep stopped grazing when she went among them. Stana, the second, was so lovely that the wolves watched the herd when she was the shepherdess. But Laptiza, the youngest, who had skin as white as milk foam and hair softer than the wool of a newborn lamb, was as beautiful as both of her sisters put together, beautiful as only she herself could be.

On a mild day in the waning summer, the three sisters went to the edge of the forest to gather strawberries. While picking through the tender green leaves, looking for the ripe fruit, they heard the tramp of galloping horses, as if an entire cavalry were rushing up. It was the emperor's son, hunting with his retainers, all handsome noble lads with erect, authoritative bearing. But the proudest of them all was the prince himself, riding the fieriest charger, a steed black as a moonless night with a white star on its forehead.

When the lads saw the sisters, they curbed their horses and circled the lasses slowly.

Listen to me, said Anna. If one of those lads should take me for his wife, I'd knead him a loaf of bread that, once he had eaten it, would make him feel always strong and brave.

And I, said Stana, would weave my husband a shirt in which he could fight against dragons and go through water without getting wet or fire without getting burned.

But I, said Laptiza, would give my husband two beautiful sons, twin boys with golden hair, and on their foreheads a golden star, brighter than the star gracing your royal charger, Highness, a star as bright as Lucifer.

Sacred be your promise, you will be mine, fairest empress, cried the emperor's son, sweeping Laptiza with her basket of berries up onto his horse.

And you will be mine! And you mine, declared two lads from the prince's retinue, each taking up a sister. So, bearing their lovely burdens on their steeds, the men dashed back to the imperial court.

The three couples were wed the next day, and for three days and nights the celebration was held throughout the empire with great pomp and splendor. After three days and nights, the news went through the whole country that Anna had gathered grain, ground, boiled, and kneaded it, and made a loaf of bread for her husband as she had promised. Then, after three more days and nights, tidings went through the land that Stana had collected flax, dried it, hackled it, and spun it into linen, wove the cloth, and made her husband a shirt as she had promised. Laptiza alone had not kept her word, but great things require time.

After seven weeks had passed, the emperor's son, now become emperor, appeared before his court with a beaming face and in a soft voice announced that he would not leave his wife's side for a long time. His heart had moved him to stay with her night and day. So the whole empire rejoiced in the expectation of seeing something never beheld before.

But many things happen in this world, among them much that is good and much that is evil.

The emperor had a stepmother, who had brought with her to the palace a daughter from her first husband whom she had intended to marry to the prince. She swore that Laptiza's promise should not come to pass, whatever had to be done. But she could not carry out her plan because the emperor remained with his wife day and night. She thought that gradually, by coaxing and cunning, she might get rid of him for long enough, but the wind blew away all her crafty words, and all her wiles were useless. As the day of fulfillment drew nearer, the stepmother felt as if the weight of a great stone were crushing the blood out of her heart. She sent a message to her brother, who ruled the neighboring kingdom, and bade him to declare war on the emperor.

This was a clever plan and not an unsuccessful one; such is the way with emperors. No matter how much they may wish to guard their families, if they hear of war, their hearts leap in their bodies, their brains swell to bursting, their eyes grow dim. Leaving wife and children in God's care, they careen into battle. So it was with our emperor. He moved as swiftly as one of God's judgments, convinced that he must do what needed to be done. He fought as only he could fight, and by the time the sun peaked in its course on the third day, he had returned to court, his heart soothed by victory and impatient to know what had happened in his absence.

This had happened: just at dawn on the morning of that third day, when the stars paled in the sky, the Lord's gift came down to the earth and Laptiza's promise was fulfilled—two beautiful princes, exactly alike, each with golden hair and a golden star on his forehead.

The world was not to see them.

The stepmother, as wicked as her thoughts, hastily put two puppies in the royal crib, in the place of the royal twins, and buried the golden-haired children at the corner of the palace, just under the emperor's windows.

When the monarch returned and saw and heard nothing but the two puppies, he wrung their necks and demanded that his wife be brought before him. No words were wasted. Despite the misgivings of his torn heart, the emperor ordered that Laptiza be buried to her breast in the earth and so remain before the eyes of the world until there was nothing left of her, in token of what befell those who tried to deceive an emperor. The next day, the stepmother's wish came to pass: the emperor married her daughter, and again the festivities lasted three days and three nights.

Yet the two princes found no rest in the earth as their mother had; two fair, beautiful aspens sprang up where their bodies were buried. When the stepmother saw the branches reaching for the emperor's window, she ordered the trees to be pulled up by the roots. The emperor replied, Let them grow. I like to see them before my window. I have never beheld such aspens before.

So the trees grew, grew as no aspens had ever grown—every day a year's growth, every night another year's growth. In the new dawn, when the stars paled in the sky, the trees shot up three years' growth in a single heartbeat. When three days and three nights had passed, the aspens were lofty and strong, shading the emperor's window with their boughs. When the wind stirred the branches, he listened to their rustling with a sweet calm in his heart.

The stepmother suspected what the trees were, and wished them gone at any cost, instructing her daughter to get her husband to have them chopped. It was a difficult task, but a woman's will can squeeze milk from a stone; a woman's cunning conquers heroes. And so it was when the empress sat upon her husband's bed and overwhelmed him with tender words and caresses, glistening tears rolling down her pink cheeks. It was a long time before the thread broke, but at last—even emperors are mortal. Very well, he said reluctantly, have your way; order the aspens to be cut down. But one must be made into a bedstead for me, the other for you.

The aspens were cut down, and before night, the beds, still lightly coated with sawdust, were standing in the emperor's room.

When the monarch lay down, he felt as if he'd become a hundred times heavier; he had never rested so well. It seemed to the empress as if she were lying on thorns and nettles, so that she could not sleep all night long. When her husband was dreaming, the beds began to creak, and amid the creaking, the wife was convinced she heard words that no one else understood.

Is it hard for you, brother? asked one of the beds.

No, it isn't hard for me. I am happy, for my beloved father rests upon me.

It's hard for me, replied the other, for on me lies a wicked soul.

When daylight came, the empress ordered two bedsteads made exactly like the ones carved from the aspens. When the emperor went hunting, she had them placed in his room without his knowledge, and threw the twin beds, down to the very smallest splinter, into a roaring fire. When they were burned so completely that not even a charcoal ember remained, she scattered the ashes to the four winds, that they might be strewn over all countries and seas, and not an atom find another atom through all eternity.

She did not notice that just when the fire was burning brightest, two flickering sparks rose, soaring upward, and fell into the deep river that flowed through the empire, where they were changed into two little fishes with golden scales, exactly alike in every aspect. One day the two fishes were scooped up in the nets of the imperial fishermen.

What pretty fishes. I have never beheld their like before, said one fisherman.

Let us take them to the emperor for a gift, said the other.

Don't take us there, said one of the fishes. We've just come from there, and going back would be our destruction.

Then what shall we do with you? asked the fishermen.

Gather dew from the leaves and let us swim in it in a sunny hollow. Don't come back again until the sun has dried the dew, said the second golden fish.

So the fishermen did as they were told—and when they returned to the clearing, what did they see?

Two boys, handsome princes with golden hair and golden stars on their foreheads, so exactly alike that no one who saw them could help knowing that they were twins. They grew rapidly, every day enough for a year, and every night enough for a year, and in the new dawn, when the stars paled in the sky, enough for three years in a single heartbeat. They grew as no children had ever grown, so that when three days and nights had passed, they were twelve years in body, twenty-four in strength, and thirty-six in wisdom.

Now let us go to our father, said one of the princes to the fishermen. The fishermen dressed the lads in what clothing they could find, rough but sturdy. They made each lad a lambskin cap, which they drew low over their heads to cover their golden hair and the golden stars upon their foreheads. The lads slipped into the palace, through the guards' fingers like quicksilver, to the great feasting hall, where the emperor was at supper. Seeing the intruders, the emperor ordered them to be seized and thrown out, the dogs set on them.

Never mind, we will go, said the princes, weeping at the harsh words, retreating down the steps. Before they could reach the gates, they were stopped by a servant who bade them to come back, as the emperor had changed his mind and wanted to see them. The princes hesitated but turned and climbed the stairs, appearing before court with their caps still on their heads. The emperor was at the head of a long, wide table, while the empress reclined beside him on twelve silk cushions. As the princes entered, one of the twelve cushions fell to the floor.

Take off your caps, cried a courtier.

To wear the head covered is a token of rank among men, replied the twins. We wish to be what we are.

The emperor might have erupted with rage, but instead he was softened by the strange music in the voices of the lads. Remain what you are, then, he answered, but who are you? Whence do you come, and what do you want?

We are twin brothers, members of a family broken in two, half in the earth, and half at the head of this table. We come whence we went, and have reached the place whence we came; we have had a long journey, have spoken in the sighing of the wind, given a voice to wood, sang in the ripples of the water. But now we wish to chant in human language a song you know without knowing it.

A second cushion fell from under the empress. Let them go home with their nonsense, she hissed to her husband.

No, let them sing, replied the emperor. I wish to hear them. Go on and sing, lads!

The empress was silent, and the princes began to sing the story of their lives:

Once upon a time something happened. Had it not happened, it would not be told. There was once an emperor who ruled over a whole world, they began, and a third cushion fell from under the empress.

When they described the emperor's departure for war, three cushions fell at once. By the time the twins had finished their song, all the cushions were felled. When they took off their caps and showed their golden hair and the golden stars on their foreheads, guests, courtiers, and the emperor himself had to close their eyes, that they might not be dazzled by so much radiance.

Irina wasn't exactly clear what this task was for, but she was pretty sure it was something unsavory. *Accessory* was a good word for what she was. Both an ornament for a body and an aid to crime. Something that was not strictly necessary, in either case.

The errand required bringing Vasilica Andreescu's passport and bank card. It was undeniably fun to slip into the skin of this nonexistent girl. Was Ms. Andreescu an orphaned heiress? Descended from vanished royalty? Why was she so young and alone with all this money? And why would she go alone to a jewelry store to buy thousands of dollars of glittering treasures for herself? Was that not a little sad, a woman alone buying jewelry for herself, without a man to gift it to her or at least a friend to offer an opinion and tell her what looked pretty? She'd wanted to bring Elena but they'd said no. They said she should ask for someone named Joseph. He would know who she is and what she is there for. She was to purchase whatever he showed her.

To be Vasilica Andreescu, Irina had chosen a ladylike pair of sling-back high heels. A knee-length dress that had something a touch Grecian about its drape, splashed with an abstract pattern in variegated shades of blue. Something sophisticated. A leather purse so soft it might have been made of baby skin—from one of Andrei's factories. One of the factories that made the genuine luxury goods, not the knockoffs.

She'd shadowed her eyes heavily with a glinting copper shade, wanting to gaze out from beneath metal lids. Her mouth shone a deep, rich red. No actress ever felt more delight at being painted for her role.

She entered the jewelry store with an air of what she hoped looked like breezy confidence. Doubtless her image would be captured on some sort of security camera. Was it possible that her image captured on a security camera was part of the point of whatever this was? Irina shivered at the sudden drop in temperature from the air-conditioning. A large U-shaped glass case took up a great deal of the smallish room, with space between it and the walls for the sales associates to move about. In the back of the room was a doorway with no door, only a gray curtain hiding what was on the other side. The lighting made the jewels dazzle; Irina didn't know where to rest her eyes. There was something she disliked about the icy clarity of the diamonds. She preferred the saturated colors of the other stones.

The solitary young woman behind the glass case smiled and asked Irina if she wanted to look at anything. Irina answered that she would like to speak with Joseph. The young woman nodded. Irina admired the gentle sway of her lovely behind in her tight pencil skirt. Was it what had gotten her this job?

From behind the curtain emerged a slender bespectacled

man whose complexion was darker than she had expected. She had expected a Russian named Iosif who had anglicized his name. Was he Gypsy like Andrei? Or some new ethnicity that she'd never seen Andrei do business with before, like an Arab or a Jew? There were some rules, set by Vasilii, about whom they could do business with. Irina was not sure whether the rules had anything to do with race.

The merchant extended his hand, shaking Irina's firmly. "Welcome, Ms. Andreescu. It is a pleasure to meet you. I am Joseph."

His slight accent did not help Irina pin down his nationality. Was he really named Yusuf, or Yosef? Something else entirely? His name was probably Joseph the way her name was Vasilica.

"Nice to meet you as well," she answered.

"I have some beautiful things for you," he said with a smile. "Let us start with the rings."

Joseph unlocked a section of the glass case and plucked two rings from a display on which several rows of them glittered. He set them lightly on a black velvet pad. Was she supposed to inspect the merchandise? Were they supposed to act as though this was a real sale for some unseen eye? She picked up one of the rings.

"This is a ruby set in white gold, with channel-set diamonds on the side," Joseph said.

Irina looked into the most thorough red she had ever seen. Blood was not red; it was practically maroon when compared with the bright flash of the large oval stone.

"Yes, beautiful," Irina commented. She opened her palm to receive the other ring after Joseph took the first one back.

"This is a lavender sapphire, set in rose gold. Look at the filigree work. The circle surrounding the base of the stone is set with diamonds all the way around. They reflect light back up into the stone, give it more fire."

Irina squinted at the tiny work. It was intricately wrought, like the gears inside an antique watch. The diamonds were so small, they were mere shards of light. The limpid purple stone's faceting lit it up in the most mesmerizing way. She looked at it in silence, forgetting whatever the situation might have prompted her to say.

"Will you take them?" Joseph asked.

"Yes," Irina answered.

"Good. Let's proceed to the necklace."

From the case, the merchant pulled out a string of pearls that he did not lay on the velvet pad but handed directly to her.

"South Sea pearls," Joseph said. "Ten millimeters. Impeccable shape and luster."

He was right: the pearls were so flawless that Irina would have guessed they were fake if it weren't for their weight in her hand. There was something about them, the way they warmed immediately to her touch, that made it clear that they had come from inside something alive. Each perfect round was the years-long work of a tortured oyster who had fashioned beauty from an impurity forced into its soft flesh. Irina liked the pearls even better than the gemstones for the suffering they had come from.

"Yes?" Joseph said.

"Yes."

"Good. Then the earrings."

How many pieces were there? From her brief glances at the price tags, she worked out that the accrued number was starting to get impressive.

The earrings were pearls set to dangle from two small gold hoops. They were the same creamy color as the necklace, with the faintest blush when given a closer look.

"Fourteen millimeters," Joseph noted.

His pitches were getting decidedly shorter and shorter. These pearls were large enough that Irina felt a real twinge of pity for the oysters. The poor things, their tender pinkness crowded within the prison of their own shells.

"That is all," Joseph said, displaying the chosen goods on the black velvet pad with satisfaction.

"You have nothing else to show me?"

"Nothing else to show you."

What a bizarre thing to say in a retail space as laden with treasure as a pirate ship.

Joseph ushered Irina into the dim room behind the gray curtain. It was a small office, with yet another entrance to some other room in the back that Irina would not be invited into. Joseph sat at the desk and tallied up the purchases.

"Your card, please, Ms. Andreescu."

He ran the card, tapping much information into the unseen screen of his computer. He printed out a paper that described each item and its price. There was a signature line. Joseph handed her a pen. For a moment, Irina considered the situation. Then she signed the false name as fluidly as she could.

"For the sake of curiosity, may I see your identification?" Joseph asked.

She handed him the passport. He looked inside, at her picture. Then her face. Then her signature on the receipt. Then the one inside the passport. "Nice," he said, as if he were congratulating her on a forgery well done. What sort of prosecutable offense had Irina just committed? She didn't even mind, when it came down to it.

She expected Joseph to give her the purchases in small, hinged boxes lined with the same black velvet as the display pad. Instead, he did something strange. He stood up and came around behind her. He encircled her neck with the pearls, gently moving her hair aside to fasten the delicate gold clasp. She felt his finger brush the back of her neck. She turned to look at him. Without a word, he picked up the earrings and clipped them to her lobes. Then he solemnly slipped the ruby on the ring finger of her left hand, and the lavender sapphire on the ring finger of her right hand, as if marrying both sides of her.

"Such pretty hands and fine fingers," he said. "You do not even need a resize."

Was this about to get unpleasant? Did he expect something from her that they had not told her about? Just as she was starting to become afraid of what might come next, Joseph smiled his tender smile and told Irina, "Go home now. It is done."

When Irina got home, Andrei was waiting. When he saw Irina laden with all the jewelry, he said, "Oh good, good. Beautiful. Very good." He laughed. "How beautiful you are, Vasilica Andreescu," he said in a loving voice without a sliver of irony. "Come to me."

She went to him and he enfolded her in his arms. He kissed her, hard, and she melted immediately. He took off her clothes the way he knew how. There must have been something uncannily delicious in the scent of him, the texture of his skin. There was no way anyone else could touch her like that, make the whole world dissolve away from her like that, leaving only the happiness of their merging. He made love to her right there on the floor of the living room, naked save for all the jewelry. She liked the weight of the pearls at her throat. She could feel the pearls swaying on the bitty hinges of her earrings, lightly resting on her jaw as she turned her head to offer him her neck to kiss. He drank from the center of her and she came until she was dizzy, drained, sated.

After, he guided her to the bedroom. As he tucked her into the plushness of their shared bed, he pulled the rings from her lax fingers, unhooked the pearls from her ears, and unfastened the pearls from her neck, performing in reverse all the gestures that Joseph had when putting these jewels on her. He put the precious things on the nightstand and slipped into the bed to sleep with her awhile. When she awoke, her lover was there next to her, his eyelids tremoring in sleep, but the precious things were gone, gone wherever it was they were supposed to go. She felt like a princess in a fairy tale who, once divested of her jewels, was a princess no longer. She was just a corrupted girl, lax and dreamy in the arms of the man who had undone her.

When Elena first tasted a Hershey bar, she wrinkled her nose. "This tastes like communist chocolate."

It took Irina a moment to absorb the assessment. "You're saying," she said, "it's not very good."

"Sorry."

"I used to love it when I was a kid. It's not like I remembered."

"Nothing is."

They threw the chocolate bars away without finishing them. There was nowhere for them to go, nothing for them to do, except find something else to buy. The men were gone doing something they would refuse to talk about once they got home. Not that the two girls were foolish enough to really want to know.

"Well, at least now I do not want chocolate anymore," Elena said, sighing.

"How do you know what communist chocolate tastes like, anyway? You're too young."

"They are my mother's words. When something was bad quality, she said it was made communist standard."

It was a warm, bright day in a series of warm, bright days—a series so long that it made Irina feel as if weather itself had vacated the area for good. There would never be cold, cloud, rain ever again. Just this endless, clear, dry season, the air motionless under the blank blue sky. The school year had ended for Irina and she was not sure that she would return to the university in the fall. She had been slowly and steadily disappearing from the life she was expected to follow. She attended fewer and fewer classes yet somehow still achieved the same middling grades, as if her education did not even need her there to accomplish itself. She'd told her parents that she was renting an apartment with some girlfriends for the summer, when really she'd moved her things into Andrei's apartment. She told her parents only lies, and somehow they let her get away with those lies. Maybe they were expecting her to be elusive as she made the slow fade into adulthood. Was it really this easy to disappear?

There was nothing to do except walk to another shop and buy another light, clingy dress to wear on another warm, bright day. Irina was not sure whether this was bliss or boredom. It was, in any case, a deviation from the bright future, the impressive career a clever girl like her was supposed to grow into.

"Does your mother know you're here in America?" Irina asked Elena.

"Yes, she wrote letters to Vasilii. She helped make the match."

Irina was on her way down, but had met Elena when she was on her way up. It was strange how lives could cross like that. Irina could have been Elena had she not been adopted by her

American parents. She could have been something a lot worse than Elena.

The two girls were in a clothing store a few streets over from the supermarket where they had bought the foul chocolate. Irina felt brief alarm at not being able to remember walking there though she clearly just had. They had wound up in the dress section on autopilot.

"Elena, what are we doing here?" Irina asked.

Elena stopped running her hand along a silk dress whose texture she was testing and laughed. "You ask the big questions!" she said merrily.

"No, I mean how did we get here from where we were ten minutes ago? I don't remember how we got here—I mean, I don't mean to ask in a cosmic way."

Maybe Irina *had* meant the question with all the grand existential angst she had tried to keep out of her voice.

"I will tell you something my mother told me when I asked her if I should marry Vasilii," Elena replied. "She said being loved by a bad man feels the best because it is a victory over all other women. Being loved by a good man feels like little because, for him, there are no other women."

"What? What does that mean?"

"Because a good man, once he has chosen you, he can have no one but you. But for a bad one, it does not matter which one you are. If he keeps you, it must be you are prettier, you are sweeter, you feel better than the others. Otherwise he would send you away and have the others. So, the love of a bad man is a greater compliment to your beauty and charm."

Irina stared at Elena wordlessly until Elena shrugged. "Maybe it makes more sense in Russian."

Irina wanted to say that no, it made perfect sense. She understood. Instead she watched Elena take a dress off the rack and hold it up to her body. It was short. Flouncy on the bottom and clingy at the bust, with spaghetti straps.

"That would bring out your pretty collarbone," Irina commented when Elena looked up at her.

"Is it possible," Elena replied, "to be bored with buying dresses? It cannot be possible." She put the dress back, the hanger clicking dryly against the metal rack.

"Has Dragos ever said anything about you to Vasilii?" Irina asked.

"What? Like what?"

"Like asked about you? Or wondered if you would do something for him?"

"Why should he? I do not think so."

So it was only Irina that Dragos wanted to purchase for sex? There must have been something specific about her that had his attention. The thought was disquieting. Or maybe Elena was playing dumb. Or Vasilii hadn't told her. Or Dragos was too afraid of Vasilii to make jokes like that about his wife. It did not mean anything that Dragos had made this quip about Irina. It wasn't personal. She could have been any woman.

Then why couldn't she shake off his strange visit that day? Why could she not forget his piercing eyes on her? Why would a nasty, crass joke out of a man who made endless nasty, crass jokes linger so? She wanted to ask Elena but did not have the courage. Not yet.

They were in the bar in the desert city, the bar with the sex show that happened downstairs in the dead of night. Irina could not help thinking of it, though it was daylight now. She wanted to ask Elena if she was thinking of the same thing. Maybe she would later, when they went to the bathroom together, away from the men. For now they listened as the men drank and talked about marriage. Not so much marriage as the wedding—not so much the wedding as the moment that makes the wedding an inevitability, that fabled moment when the man proposes. A pretty image from a fairy tale.

"It does not matter what film stock," Dragos explained, "the image is always the same. It can be black and white, silent. It can be the most beautiful colors of the most expensive Hollywood production. It does not matter. There is always Vaseline on the lens. There are violins swelling. Even if the acting is bad, stiff like for a porno, the image is always the same. They are young, they are beautiful, the man and the girl, having dinner at a nice restaurant."

"With a starched white tablecloth," Andrei said, "and some candles."

"Yes, and they look into each other's eyes as if they are asleep with love—"

"Catatonic is the word," Andrei interrupted, "and they have just eaten some rich dessert with chocolate."

"Yes," Dragos continued, "the same chocolate dessert that will make the pretty girl into a fat wife in five years. And there is champagne too. And the girl laughs when the bubbles tickle her nose. And something hard hits her in the teeth when she takes a drink. She catches the thing in her hand and we know what comes next but, the silly girl, she does not. She almost faints when the man gets down in front of her on one knee. She opens her hand and he takes the ring from her, takes the ring from her palm and slips it on her small, dainty finger. The diamond is gigantic and perfect. The girl cries from joy."

"What could be better?" Andrei laughed. "The man has finally made the girl a woman!"

"What a beautiful image, no? Is that how it was, Vasilii?" Dragos quipped. "Is that how it was when you made Elena your woman?"

"That beautiful image," Vasilii answered placidly, "has a fray in the corner. Do you see? Pull a little and the music stops. Pull some more and you see that it is laid on top of something else, another image."

Irina was waiting so intensely for Vasilii to finish his thought that she did not see that someone had come up to their table until Vasilii looked up at this person, nodding a curt greeting.

"Sorry it's a little late, Mr. Grigoriev," the man said, handing over a black leather briefcase. The careful way he handled it made it look substantially heavy. His face was familiar. For several seconds, Irina could not place him. Then she remembered. He was from downstairs. He was the man with the dolphin tattoo who may or may not have winked at her before he finished his performance in his partner's mouth. Irina's blood rushed up to make her cheeks blaze. It had taken her several seconds to identify the man's face, but had he appeared before her naked, she would have recognized him immediately.

Irina looked at Elena to see her reaction, but there was none. The girl's face was blank. Vasilii grunted something like an assent after putting the briefcase on the table in front of him and waved the man off. The messenger excused himself with a small awkward bow.

"Good," Dragos said. "I thought the delivery might have been held up again."

The pebbled leather on the briefcase looked even more familiar than the face of the man with the dolphin tattoo. Was it the very same one that had been brought to the hotel suite on the day she had been given Vasilica Andreescu's passport?

Once again, Irina laid her hand on it. She was going to find out what was in there this time.

"I would not open that if I were you," Vasilii said flatly.

"And why not?" Irina looked straight into his pale eyes, but it was Andrei who answered her question.

"So that when the judge asks you what was in the case, you will not have to lie when you tell him you do not know," he said.

Dragos smiled as if this were all very amusing, while Vasilii remained stone-faced. Irina, undeterred, opened the latch on the briefcase with a loud snap. Nobody had time to respond before she had the briefcase open. It was packed tightly with bricks of white powder wrapped in cellophane. She saw them for only an instant before Vasilii's flat, angry hand quickly pushed the case shut on its silent silvery hinges. He nearly crushed her fingers in the mouth of the case.

The look on his face was unlike anything she had ever seen. The clear cold of the purest Arctic ice. No. It was beyond that. Purer and colder than anything of this earth. It was something from outer space. Absolute zero. For several heartbeats, nobody moved. Then Elena took Irina quickly by the shoulder and announced in an awkwardly loud voice, "Time for us ladies to visit the powder room!"

"Are you crazy?" Elena hissed once they were alone in the echoing, black marble bathroom. "Do you want to get us all killed?"

The bathroom had mirrors up to the ceiling. In all the repeated reflections of the two girls, their bodies looked small and vulnerable. Elena's hair had a vaguely electrified look, as if what Irina had done had literally shocked her.

"Well, now I know," Irina said. "Drugs."

She had seen what Andrei trafficked. There were luxury goods. Cars. Now drugs. She wondered if he also had a hand in the business of women.

"Did you see that guy who delivered the briefcase?" Irina asked.

"Irina, you must want to die."

Elena looked up at her friend wearily, and for the first time that evening it struck Irina how tired she looked. The tender skin under her eyes had darkened to a bruise-like blue. Her pallor seemed starker than ever. But perhaps it was only the light in the bathroom that gave Elena's face its sepulchral appearance.

"Well, didn't you recognize him?"

"I am supposed to recognize him?" Elena answered, rooting around in her minuscule purse.

"It was the guy," Irina explained. "From the sex show. With the dolphin tattoo. Elena, are you okay?"

"Why should I not be okay? My only friend tries to get us all killed and everything is okay."

Irina didn't know how to answer. Elena's sarcastic anger was a red-hot flare. And yet she had also just told Irina that she was her only friend.

"How are things with Vasilii?" Irina ventured gently.

"He is my husband. He does not talk to me much except to give me orders."

Irina had not thought before of Vasilii's long pianist's hand raised against her frail friend, but suddenly this seemed a possibility. If everyone became paralyzed with terror when some upstart orphan dared to openly flout him, what was he like in private with a woman that he owned? "He doesn't hurt you, does he?"

"Ha! No, not where you can see it."

Irina looked Elena over for bruises not quite hidden by liquid makeup.

"Irina!" Elena said with some exasperation. "Don't look at me like that. He does not beat me. He is a fine husband. He is kind to me."

The affirmation of Vasilii's kindness sounded so hollow that Irina winced. Of course Elena knew that Irina heard the falseness of it. Yet she was telling her friend in the only way she knew how to back off.

"You'd tell me now if something really bad was going on?" Irina said. It was the only way she knew how to tell her friend to come to her when she could, when she needed to.

Elena did not look into Irina's face when she nodded yes. Instead of making eye contact, she went back to rooting around in her purse. "Where is the damn lipstick? How could I lose anything in this stupid tiny bag?" she said. "It's no bigger than my fist!"

"Here, use mine," Irina offered.

Elena accepted Irina's lipstick in her upturned hand. After she had reddened her mouth and pinched a paper towel with her lips to set the color, she asked Irina if Andrei would marry her one day.

"I don't know that he would ask me such a thing," Irina answered. "I don't know if I would, even if he did."

When the two girls came out of the bathroom, their mouths freshly glossed with the same berry shade, the men were hunched toward one another, speaking in hushed tones. When they saw the girls, they settled back into their seats. Dragos asked Vasilii with a fake casualness that embarrassed everybody, "So, what was the image?"

"What?"

"The image that was under the pretty proposal picture once you peeled it back."

"Ah. I forget." Vasilii shrugged. "Snow. Just snow."

"White and cold and unmarred as the purest bride," Dragos said, clinking the bottom of his glass of vodka against the top of Vasilii's, which was untouched on the table.

Irina pressed herself to Andrei on the booth seat. "Andrei," she whispered urgently in his ear, "we are all of us criminals."

"Now now, darling," he answered quietly, gently squeezing her hand. "We are only capitalists."

Then he turned to the other men, attempting another toast to distract Vasilii. "To capitalism!" he said with boozy gusto.

Dragos burst into laughter and raised his glass once again. "To American toilet paper!"

"What? What for?" Elena asked.

"Because," Andrei explained, "Romanian toilet paper is worse than you can possibly imagine. Worse than even your Soviet husband can imagine. It is like wiping your ass with dry leaves and despair."

This made Vasilii crack a small smile, and deign to respond with his own toast, "Yes, to America." He clicked his glass against Irina's, which had been refilled in her absence. "To America, where you can wipe your ass with a cloud!"

Irina picked up her glass to take a drink as she was expected to, to accept what must have been Vasilii's gesture of reconciliation. She could have sworn, when she felt the clear heat of the alcohol flood her mouth, that Dragos—the bastard—winked at her with something like complicity, as if the two of them were about to play a fine trick on everyone.

Cinci

What is the image? There is no image yet. Only white. You notice it's ever so slightly frayed at the corner, see? Pull a little and it peels up. Pull some more, it makes a sound like tape being torn, and expose what is beneath, still dewy and crinkled and unsure of the light like a butterfly unfurling from its chrysalis. More white! Snow. Covering the ground as far as the eye can see, sometimes stirring itself in rising whorls when the wind breathes on it, and there, in the distance, galloping in from the horizon—a Phanariot. Does it matter which one? It hardly does. One of the thirty-three who ruled over Moldavia or one of the thirty-five who ruled over Wallachia. Perhaps he ruled over one and was moved to the other. It doesn't matter now, now that he rides alone through endless wastes of icy nothing. At least he was not one of the ones who were executed. Exile, for this one.

Not Moldavian and not Wallachian. Certainly not this thing that will not exist for at least another century, Romanian. He speaks several languages, but not whatever it is they speak. He is a Greek sent by Turks. Somehow both Byzantine and Ottoman. Touched by Russia. Sent in great pomp by the court barely two years before to rule over the principality he had purchased from the Porte. He owed many creditors for his great bribe. It is possible that the taxes he levied on the peasants to pay back this debt were too heavy. He does not think of this. It is not the peasants, after all, who cast him out. It was the machinations of the court, impatient with his tributes not being high enough. It was the boyars, only too glad to get rid of him, all of them dreaming of taking his place.

He is convinced that if he stops moving, he will die. His frozen body would never be found. They did not let him keep a proper coat against this stunningly bitter winter, not even a hat. A stable boy gave him a large scarf of rough, undyed wool on the way out. It is a pretty, deep cream color, but dirty. He has to wrap his head in it like a woman, against the cold. At least they let him keep a good horse. A young, strong animal—he can feel the life shivering through its limbs. The Phanariot is no stranger to riding. The wind has carved deltas by the eyes of his sun-browned face. Or are they lines from frowning at belligerents? Smiling at court entertainments? You'd have to look at his mouth to tell, to see whether it is sweet or sour, but you cannot see. It is covered by the scarf.

They called him hospodar. But they would not call him voivode. He is not very old at all, not as old as he looks.

Hunger drills him. He needs to find some small animal, pull out its steaming guts under the blank blue sky. He needs to eat tonight. But he has no gun. They left him only a knife. How can he get close enough to something to kill it? He takes out his knife; it flashes in the heatless sun. There are riders in the East who are known to cut tiny pieces of flesh from their horses' shoulders while mounted on them. He thinks of sucking a chunk of bloody, quivering meat from the edge of his blade. He cannot do it for now. He likes the horse too much. But if he does not feel something solid and warm in his mouth he will die.

How long has it been? Not very long at all. And yet it seems hard for his numbed brain to remember a time when the living was easy, when skin left unwrapped by furs did not hurt from the cold, turn black, turn dead. There must have been mildness and plenty but, already, he cannot be sure. The memory could be false. He might have dreamed it. He rides south, praying to get away from this winter. Will there be a place to sleep tonight? Will there be firelight?

He has not seen many women out here, and what women there are tell rough stories and dirty jokes in a language he can barely piece together, wear animal pelts and grainy wool, snap the necks of the animals they eat with their bare hands. The men must love them the same blunt way he loves his horse.

When they called him hospodar but never called him voivode, there was a girl with a gentle laugh and skin like milk who wore silks in more colors than he knew existed in our dim world. He could never pay enough for her garments, such miracles they were on her. She unfurled her dresses for him and preened, more satisfied with herself than the showiest male bird in the springtime—the springtime, he knows, does not come from above from the sun as they say. He knows it comes from below, when desire rises from the molten core of earth and the ice must yield, turn liquid. The ground cracks its own white carapace, pierces itself with green shoots—and the girl fits her dresses over her supple body, asking, aglow with the yearning to please, Do you like this one or this one?

Oh, they are both beautiful but please stay naked, my dear. Better this way.

What did they do with her? Did they slit her throat? Did they send her away? Did they take her for themselves? Did she cry for him? Or does it not matter which prince buys her the dresses?

Even out in this killing cold, there is beauty. The other night he emerged from dark bush to see the full moon enormous and white, rising low just over the bare trees. Its sudden appearance cut his breath—then just as his mouth rounded into a silent O, a wolf howled and howled and howled.

The girl had extraordinary hair that draped in lush wavy cascades over his plush pillows. A honeyed color not quite brown not quite blonde that gleamed red in the firelight. He liked the way she yelped when he gripped it while riding her. He knows that his yearning for the girl will make him suffer more than his evaporated gold coins, his pulverized titles, his vanished retinue. Lack of her will make him suffer more than the cold. He tells himself she does not exist. Or if she ever existed she is dead. From that time before, already he cannot remember. That time before the cataclysm, before the whiteout.

But he must ride on. If there is one thing life has taught him, it's that the only way out is through. Toward the spring. Toward the horizon. The vanishing line. Is the soft, blurry image of the girl what makes him want to go still and wait for death or is it the only thing pushing him on? Is the pain of not having her the only thing that can reach through the cold, and needle him alive?

Andrei didn't like to talk about where he came from. He especially didn't want to talk about his father. "There's nothing to tell," he'd say. "He was an itinerant. All I have of him is the brown skin that made me a dirty Gypsy. It is a wonder that my mother did not give her shame away to an orphanage. It must be some people like to keep their shame with them."

He'd try to turn the conversation away, back toward Irina. He'd say, "It begs the question why your mother would give you away, darling. A lovely white baby like you. Where's the shame in that?"

"Maybe she was poor. Maybe she couldn't afford me."

"Yes, well, most everybody is poor. Poor and desperate and hungry and can't do a damn thing about it."

He said this in such a way that she suspected he didn't envision the poverty strictly in a physical sense. It wasn't just about drafty hovels and small portions of bad food, never enough to satisfy. Having to fight the elements every day to stay alive, to stay sane. Trying to remain convinced that what you did mattered at all, that you shouldn't let go and keep falling, keep falling forever. After all, perhaps it was hard to determine where physical poverty turned into whatever Andrei was getting at. Moral poverty? Even that phrase seemed too glib, too small to contain it. Whatever it was, it had to do with loneliness. Connections that were either severed or never formed with a world that didn't care.

Whoever Andrei's father was, wherever he was, he was old by now. Shriveled and toothless, probably. Dead, possibly. Certainly no longer a dashing vagabond who seduced village maidens and then careened off to other adventures, leaving the maidens unmaidened, suddenly weighed down with all the burdens of womanhood. A dark child with gray eyes. How can a woman so fiercely love what has ruined her? The body, the body has its ways. The body hates being discrete. It wants to impinge and be impinged upon. It wants to open up and adulterate itself. The swollen breast aches to nurture the bastard baby of the man who left. There's nothing to be done about it.

Dissolve—dissolve is the word. The day they met, Irina had told Andrei that the spent carcasses of dead cicadas *decomposed* into the earth to feed their brood, they did not *dissolve*. But *dissolve* is the right word after all for what the body wants to do. It wants to melt into another body until everything becomes indistinguishable, until the two bodies merging are gone, leaving in their place an amalgam. Something like a unity.

"Why are you so keen on knowing about my parents anyway?" Andrei asked. "You have two sets of your own: the ones that made you and didn't want you and the ones that didn't make you and wanted you. That ought to keep you philosophically occupied for the rest of your life!"

"You never talk about your family. Don't you ever write them?"

"Why would I do that? I became a lot less interesting after my mother managed to make some poor sot marry her and had some proper white children."

"Come on. They'd want to know about you. Everywhere you've been. All the money you made."

"Ha! As if that would make them forgive my impurity."

"Your not being white, you mean."

"That is a better way to put it. Purity is a bullshit idea for fairy tales. No, wait, that is an insult. No self-respecting fairy tale is simple enough to believe in purity."

He laughed then, laughed the pointed way he always laughed at things that were dubiously funny. Dubious was his favorite brand of humor. How did a ramshackle device like Andrei manage to keep functioning in any way at all, and why did Irina stay to falter with him? He was the ultimate bad choice. He was a mockery of the rational. He was the gaping maw of the bad dream Irina didn't want to wake up from, because letting him eat her alive felt so much more vivid than being awake.

She liked to let him paint her face. She liked the feel of the plush brush against her skin; she liked the expectation in his eyes. She laid out her lipsticks for him in a neat row and asked, "What color do you want my mouth?" He picked a plum shade that would shortly be smeared all over him. She didn't know why doing this made him hard for her yet she helplessly responded, felt the blood rise to her cheeks to meet the powder blush he was applying there. Pink on pink, impossible to tell the real arousal apart from the cosmetic mimicking it.

She might have been disturbed by his predilection for making her up: the scene was reminiscent of an undertaker carefully making up a corpse. The thought of her own death sank into her flesh like the warmth from a bath. It was not frightening. There was even a strange sort of comfort in it. One day a man might paint her face with her no longer behind it—it would have ceased being her face, the features hollowed into a mask that looked like what had once been her.

For now, she was there, alive, stock-still, looking up at the man who was painting another woman's face on top of her bare face. He was doubling her. Or he was overwriting her. He was inscribing her into her own body. She was woman and woman was she.

When he lined her eyes, her lids didn't even quiver. Not because she trusted him not to hurt her with the pencil—his hand was, after all, trembling slightly—but because a hurt inflicted by his hand was the best hurt of all.

The whole thing must have started with the fight with Andrei. Or something like a fight. It was impossible to goad that man into an earnest, straightforward confrontation. Their arguments were always couched in ridiculous hypotheticals, innuendo, shards of ironic philosophy. It was all in jest, until gradually it wasn't. Irina asked Andrei why he would make a joke about whoring her to Dragos. Andrei fixed her with his dark gray eyes and demanded to know, "Do you want to be whored to Dragos?"

"Why would you ask a thing like that?"

"Well, do you want to? It would be easy enough."

"So what if I do? So what if I do—" She laughed the laugh he had taught her, the laugh that wasn't really a laugh.

Because neither one of them was willing to stop and be serious, here she was at last in Dragos's plush bed, still disbelieving her nakedness. He was smoking a cigarette and staring at her with an expression she did not recognize. She would have expected him to be smirking, maybe even glowing with victory, but that was not the look on his face.

"He was right," Dragos said. "What a sweet, snug, friendly little cunt you have."

Of course, they were both thinking of Andrei. Dragos's voice was strange and dreamy, like a man gazing into an oracular mirror. It was decidedly un-Dragos-like. The usual Dragos would have gotten out of bed with a hearty chuckle and fetched Irina a nice brick of tidy cash to pass on to her man. But at the moment, there was no question of bringing up the ten thousand dollars. There was no question of pantomiming the joke all the way to its conclusion. The transaction that had just taken place was not entirely unpleasant. Irina hadn't cried or cursed God. She had, somehow, even forgotten about Andrei while Dragos was inside her; she had been in the moment. She'd attempted to observe the intensity that was happening, but perhaps the intensity at hand was the intensity of her observation itself. It was all very circular. Or possibly expansive. Was she looking at Dragos? Or herself? Or something other? Or were they both turned toward this something other together?

"This is stupid," Irina said.

"What? What, what we just did?"

"No."

He looked relieved at the speed of her answer. She thought for a moment before speaking again. "I guess what I am feeling. What I am feeling is stupid. Oh, I don't know. Never mind me, really."

Dragos looked her over as if evaluating her. "You will not stay with us long," he said.

"Well, I have all afternoon."

"No, with us three. With Andrei and me and Vasilii. At least, you should not stay with us much longer. Whatever it is we have to teach, I think you have already learned it."

Irina looked at him. His cigarette smoke whorled lazily in the air between them, its acridity slightly stinging her eyes. Decidedly, people act in strange ways once you have sex with them. The image that you had of them peels back and reveals another image.

Dragos averted his eyes and cleared his throat. His voice was a little dimmed when he asked, "Did Andrei tell you what happened at the garage last week?"

"No, he seldom talks about work."

"He should have told you. It's a funny story."

"Well then go ahead and tell me instead of playing the demure girl," she said, imitating his inflection and accent. There was a certain pleasure in mocking a man she suspected was a killer. Like putting her hand in a crocodile's mouth, daring it to leave her whole.

Dragos did not take offense; he merely told her about one night when he and Andrei were at the garage late, doing some accounting. Irina had never even seen the warehouse, but imagined it to be large, gray, and imposing. The shipment had just gone out, so the garage was not filled with the usual cars built from other cars. Dark emptiness, like the mind of a murderer. Except for one car. Dragos's vintage red sports coupe, a sleek, unreliable machine that he loved precisely because it cost him so much money to maintain, as if its mercurial temperament enhanced its beauty. A skinny young lad dressed all in black, his face scarred by acne, was attempting unsuccessfully to jimmy his way inside the roadster. So absorbed was he by his work that he did not even notice Andrei and Dragos until he was grabbed by the back of his hoodie.

"You know, even if you get in there, the bitch probably won't start up," said Dragos pleasantly.

The lad screamed, dropping the twisted wire he was attempting to shove into the lock.

"You really ought to be more vigilant, in your line of work," Andrei remarked helpfully. The lad was breathing fast, not yet trying to wrench free from Andrei's grasp but calculating how to do so. His filmy eyes darted wildly. Probably, he was on some kind of substance, something less mellow than what Dragos gave his women. It was to be hoped that his faculties were impaired, Dragos explained when he told Irina the story; the thought of his being naturally that stupid was too depressing. What the lad decided to do in order to extricate himself from the situation was puff himself up. He said he had connections, that Andrei and Dragos better let him go or they could get themselves killed. He was really important. They would regret this.

"This is adorable," said Andrei to Dragos. "This is just precious."

The lad said he was associated with Vasilii Grigoriev, and that Grigoriev would not like to hear about his unjust detainment. At least, that was what they could make out through his word salad. It was even harder to follow what he was getting at once they started to laugh at him.

"So, you received permission from Grigoriev himself to rob his warehouse?" Andrei smiled.

"Permission from—what?"

"You are in Grigoriev's warehouse right now, son."

The lad blanched visibly. "No," he said. "No, you lie."

"I assure you we have no reason to."

"You lie! He will peel the skin off your balls with a pocket-knife and make you eat it. He is a good friend of mine—he is a cousin."

"Well, we can sort this out with a single call," said Andrei. He passed the lad to Dragos like a sack of potatoes and took his cell phone from his pocket.

"You shitheads," the lad said, sneering. "The cops won't fuck with me. Grigoriev owns the cops."

"I am not calling the police," Andrei explained, "but our friend Vasilii himself."

"You lie! You don't know him. *I* know him!"

When Vasilii picked up and was told of the situation, he seemed mildly amused. He asked to speak to the lad in question. Andrei held the phone up to his ear. The lad was trembling now, muttering his name almost inaudibly into the receiver. When he looked straight into Andrei's eyes with an imploring expression, Andrei took the phone back and heard Vasilii's neutral voice say, "I do not know this boy. He is not even a cousin of a friend of a cousin of a friend. You may dispose of him."

"Dispose of him?"

"You have your gun, no?"

"It's not here."

Dragos overheard and offered, "We could garrote him with his wire."

"For fuck's sake, Dragos, you feel like staying here and scraping this idiot's DNA off the pavement for the next hour?" Andrei said tetchily. "It would be disgusting. And I'm fucking tired."

"All right, I'll send someone," Vasilii said agreeably, and hung up.

While they waited, the lad changed his escape strategy to abject groveling. He begged to be let go, cried like a little girl. A little mucus bubble burst out of his nostril while he sobbed. It was a sorry spectacle.

"What if we let him out?" Andrei asked.

"Ah no, if somebody shows up and we have no one to take away, Vasilii will not like it."

It was not even five minutes before a silent black sedan crept into the warehouse. Which was a good thing because the hysterical crying was giving Dragos a headache and he was liable to punch the lad in the face. Two men exited the car and pushed a gun against the side of the lad's head. The tears ran fat and crooked over his ugly, scarred cheeks. That was the last Dragos and Andrei saw of him, being forced into the car Vasilii had sent, to be taken care of elsewhere.

"Where did they take him?" Irina asked when Dragos went silent.

"Who knows?" Dragos said. "Wherever Vasilii said."

Irina was going to ask if the lad was dead, but what was the point when Dragos had not seen a body, didn't know for sure? In the face of such uncertainty, she could imagine whatever she liked. She could imagine they conked him over the head and left him on the outskirts of town, that he woke up the next morning with a wicked migraine and a small spot of dried blood on his brow. Just enough blood to signify injury but not enough to be worrisome; just the sort of cosmetic wound the hero would receive in an action movie. Which would turn into a tidy white scar to tell girlfriends about later, some sexy dangerous story in which he was not an idiot, did not cry, acquitted himself well.

Dragos watched Irina think for a bit, and then said musingly, "You know, at the root of human morality is empathy and the belief in meaning. Criminals suffer a lack of at least one of these two things. The likes of Andrei and I, we do not believe anything means anything, and so we are free."

"What about the empathy part?" Irina wanted to know. "Do you have any of that?"

"Ha!" Dragos sneered. "If I answered that question, I would reveal a weakness, no matter what the answer. I cannot disclose that, darling, for security reasons."

He'd called her "darling," just like Andrei. Andrei was the one they had fucked. He might as well have been in the room, watching them. Maybe he had been. Maybe Andrei and Dragos were really just two pieces of the same person.

Andrei was in a possessive rage once Dragos was done with Irina. His face was violently flushed, his body tight and trembling with rage. He looked as if he had been pacing the apartment like a murderous animal in a cage.

"Was he any good?" he demanded to know the moment she stepped through the front door. She didn't know how to answer, so she stood there staring at him stupidly, like transfixed prey.

"I said, was he a good fuck?" Andrei repeated, a little louder.

"I don't know," she answered quietly. "What's a bad fuck like?"

"If you don't know that, clearly you haven't fucked enough people."

Irina closed the door. She tried to walk past him. He caught her by the arm. "I bet you still have his smell on you."

"I'm going to take a shower, right now," she said dryly.

"No, leave him on you." He pulled her against him, his grip digging into her upper arms. "Are you still my girl, now, under the stench of him?"

"It wasn't my idea to go over there."

"You're a whore now. You're not my girl."

She looked into his red face and dared him. "Why don't you see if you can make me? Make me your girl again."

He kissed her, hard, to stop her mouth from uttering another word. It was not only her he was furious at; it seemed it was everything. He vibrated with desire to destroy the whole world. But all he had in his arms at the moment was this frail female body, and she would have to do.

They fucked across the apartment like a pair of raving animals, shedding hastily removed clothes along the way. The couch, the floor, up against a wall. Eventually they were on the bed, she at the edge of it on her back, he standing over her holding her legs apart, boring himself into her as viciously as he knew how. She ground back against him, moaning through gritted teeth. He reached for her neck and squeezed just above the clavicle. The pressure of his hand was not yet meant to hurt, but it was insistent enough to remind Irina that it could.

"Whore!" he spat, which made her laugh. She laughed and came at the same time so that her body did not at all know what noise to make—she was left gasping, mouth agape, trembling from head to toe.

"What's so funny?" Andrei demanded. "What's so fucking funny?"

"I am not a whore, Andrei. He hasn't paid me yet so I am only a slut."

At those words the grip on her neck tightened. He had both hands around her throat and was choking her in earnest. She went into a hot, overwhelming swoon until he finished. She watched him with her dimming eyes. He reared when he came in that way that she loved, as if his body was shocked and overwhelmed at the pleasure she gave. He groaned her name and collapsed. She held him to her with her eyes closed, feeling new air penetrating her lungs, slowly bringing her back. She kissed his ear before she whispered into it, "What does it matter, anyway? Have you not been inside more women than I can count on fingers and toes?"

"It's not the same," Andrei said, with something like sated exhaustion.

"How is it not the same?"

"It's not the same because you are a woman, darling. It's just not the same."

She supposed he was right. It was true that being a woman complicated things, that it was costlier. It wasn't fair but it was true. She nuzzled the bite mark she had left on his shoulder. He petted her long, tangled hair.

"How many of them were bad fucks?" Irina asked.

"I don't know. Not most, but a significant portion. Sometimes it might have been my fault too. I don't know. A bad fuck is like…a bad fuck is when the other touches you and you think it would be more interesting to look over your bank books to see how much money you have."

Irina looked at Andrei until he shook his head. "Never mind. You are too young to know. That is why you are so good. That is why I cannot keep myself from ruining you."

The idea that a woman could be ruined, like a white silk dress with red wine spilled on it—was this one of his jokes? His face looked peaceful. His eyes were half-lidded as if heavy with satisfaction. His lips were lax as if his mouth had devoured a whole world. She wanted to ask him why a man would hand off his girl to another man. It must have been more than something between her and Andrei. It must have been something between him and Dragos, some man thing. A drive for competition, for showing each other up? Or maybe even a perverse kind of love, like breaking bread together. Maybe it was some sort of Romanian thing. If she asked about that, surely Andrei would dismiss her immediately. He preferred, whenever possible, not to talk about Romanian things.

Still, while she had him there in her arms, she had to ask, "Andrei? Remember that story you told me with the lamb?"

"Yes. Miorița."

"Why would the shepherd let his enemies kill him if he knew they meant to? Why wouldn't he try to avert his own death?"

Andrei didn't answer right away. She waited for his reply in stubborn silence.

"Irina, that is an American question you are asking."

He sounded a touch impatient and vaguely disappointed, as if he'd expected better from her. This was funny coming from a man who so casually took everything he wanted. If stoic passivity was a Romanian trait, he wasn't very good at being Romanian. In that way, he was actually more American than she was.

What story did she fit into? Many stories lived in her head, but she couldn't find one that would explain her to herself. Maybe that was the thing, she half-thought, half-dreamed as she drifted off to sleep while bruises shaped like Andrei's fingers bloomed into being all over her body. Maybe she wasn't really a person. She was just stories mashed together in the shape of a girl.

After Dragos told her the story about the garage, Irina thought their encounter was over. She thought she'd get dressed and go home, now that he'd gotten up to fetch himself a stiff drink. When he came back, he had the clear heat of vodka on his breath.

"You're a bad influence on me with that sweet slit of yours," he said. "You have me drinking in the early afternoon."

"Well, it's not like you *have* to drink. We could just fuck."

"Ha! The wisdom of the young."

He was hard again. When Irina tried to get up, he reached for her and gathered her to himself.

"Again?" she said, compelled yet unsure about the wisdom of another round.

"Why not? You said you have all afternoon."

"Shit. Why did I say that?"

He lasted longer this time, so she had the leisure to pay closer attention to him. When he'd first been inside her, she was too excited and distraught that he was not Andrei to notice exactly what about him was different than the man she belonged to. Now she could observe the different shape, the different weight of him. His hand on her, broader and with squatter fingers. The different way it handled her. And yet there was a sameness there.

"You know," Dragos said after he had once again finished, "if you are hanging around us because you are trying to understand some Romanian thing, some *thing* about your origins, I do not know if we can help with that."

"Well. You ought to be able to, since you're both from there."

"I rather think I am from nowhere."

"Now there's a bunch of manly bullshit. Everyone is from somewhere, especially men with as much baggage as you."

"All right, then I am generally baggaged, but not baggaged in a Romanian way."

"Come on."

"Come on yourself!"

"Come on. I'll show you. Tell me a Romanian story."

"A what? How does a woman go asking for a thing like that? Usually they ask for more pills, not for fucking fairy tales."

"Tell me a Romanian story. Now. Even if it's one about how you can never go home again."

Patru

Once upon a time something happened. Had it not happened, it would not be told. There was once a mighty emperor and empress who were unable to have children. They went to many diviners, witches, and philosophers, but for a long time all was in vain. Then one day the royal court visited the hut of an old man renowned for his wisdom, and the old man told the emperor, Your wish will bring you sorrow.

I am not here to question you about that, replied the emperor, but to learn whether you have any plants to give us that will bestow the blessing of children.

I have, but you will possess only one child. He will be a handsome, lovable boy, yet you will not be able to keep him long.

So the child was born, but from the hour of his birth he screamed in a way no magic arts could silence. The emperor held the wailing baby and promised him all the good things the world contained, without being able to quiet him: Hush, little lad, I will give you the most beautiful princess in the world for your wife. Hush, my son, I will give you kingdoms spanning beyond the known world.

Finally, the emperor, dazed with too little sleep and unaware of the meaning of the words he cooed at his son, said, Hush now, my boy, and I will give you youth without age and life without death.

At that moment, the little prince stopped crying and looked up at his father with limpid, hopeful eyes. The emperor was awash with dread.

The older the boy grew, the more thoughtful and reflective he became. Tutored by the best philosophers, he excelled at every sort of learning so that the emperor died of joy and came to life again. The whole realm was proud of having a prince so wise and learned, a second King Solomon. But one day, when the lad had just reached his fifteenth year and the emperor sat at a banquet with the nobles of the country, the handsome prince rose, saying, Father, the time has come. You must now give me what you promised at my birth.

When the emperor heard this he grew sorrowful and answered: Why, my son, how can I give you an impossible thing? If I promised it to you then, it was only to hush you.

If you can't give it to me, father, I shall be obliged to wander through the whole world till I find what was promised to me, and for which I was born.

The young hero went to the imperial stables, where the finest steeds in the realm were standing, to choose one of them. But all the horses bucked and neighed at his touch, save one sick, weak horse in the corner, covered with sores. What do you command, my master? said the animal. I thank God that He has permitted a hero's hand to touch me once more.

I intend to go on a journey to seek youth without age and life without death.

To obtain your wish, the horse replied, you must ask your father for the sword, lance, bow, quiver of arrows, and garments he wore when a youth. Also, you must take care of me with your own hands for six weeks and give me oats boiled in milk.

The prince rummaged through his father's old chests, finding at the bottom of a trunk the weapons and garments his father had worn in his youth, but the arms were covered with rust. He set to work cleaning them with his own hands and in six weeks, during the time he was taking care of the horse, he succeeded in making the weapons glint like mirrors. When the horse heard from the handsome prince that the clothes and arms were cleaned and ready, he shook himself once. All the sores instantly fell off and there the horse stood, a strong, well-formed animal, with four wings. May you have a long life, master. From today I shall be at your service, the horse declared.

When the court saw the lad ready to set off, clad in the emperor's restored battle vestments, all implored him to give up the journey and not risk his life. When the emperor saw that his son's resolve would not be shaken, he granted the prince a retinue of two hundred horsemen and a string of carts loaded with provisions and money. He watched the lad set spurs to his steed and dash away through the gate like the wind, the old familiar dread in the pit of his stomach.

After reaching the boundaries of his father's country and breaching the wilderness, the prince distributed all his property among the escort, bade them farewell, and sent them back, keeping for himself only as much food as the horse could carry.

Turning east, he rode for three days and three nights, till he came to a wide plain where lay a great many human bones.

You must know, said the horse, that we are on the land of the Woodpecker Fairy, who is so wicked that nobody who enters her domain ever comes out again. She was once a woman, but the curse of her parents, whom she angered with her disobedience, turned her into a woodpecker. She is terribly big, but don't be frightened. Keep your sword and bow at the ready.

No sooner had the horse spoken than a terrible howl came from the tree line on the horizon, and the Woodpecker Fairy crashed out of the woods, knocking down trees and blasting bones to dust as she roared across the plain at our prince. The horse leapt up like the wind over the charging nemesis while the prince shot off one of her feet with an arrow. Just as he was pulling another arrow from his quiver, the fairy cried, Stop, young hero. I'll do you no harm.

Seeing that he did not believe her, she gave him the promise written with her own blood. Your horse cannot be killed, my young hero, she explained. It is enchanted. If it hadn't been for that, I would have roasted and eaten you. Know that until today no mortal man has ventured to cross my boundaries as far as this. The few bold knights who attempted it reached only the plain where you saw so many bones.

They now went to the fairy's house, where she entertained them as guests. The clement prince fastened her severed foot back onto her leg, and the wound instantly healed. The hostess, in her joy, kept open house for three days, and begged the emperor's son to choose one of her beautiful daughters for his wife. He would not do that, but told her what he was seeking, and she replied, With your horse and your heroic courage, I believe you will succeed.

At the end of his sojourn, the prince took his leave and rode on and on. When he finally crossed the frontiers of the Woodpecker Fairy's kingdom, he entered a beautiful meadow, one side of which was covered with blooming plants, while the other side was scorched earth. When the prince asked why the grass was singed off the ground, the horse answered, We are now in the domain of the Scorpion Witch; she is the Woodpecker Fairy's sister, but they are both so wicked that they can't live together. Their parents' curse has fallen upon them, and so, as you see, they have become monsters. Their enmity goes beyond all bounds; they are always trying to get possession of each other's lands. When this one is angry, she spits fire and pitch; this scorched earth here must be the remains of a border skirmish. This witch is even worse than her sister, and has three heads.

No sooner had the horse spoken than a crackling hiss filled the air unlike anything ever heard before. The Scorpion Witch, with one jaw in the sky and the other on the earth, approached like the wind, spitting fire as she came, but the horse darted upward swiftly while our hero shot an arrow, felling one of her heads. When he was going to strike off another, the Scorpion Witch entreated him to forgive her, she would do him no harm, and to convince him of this she gave him her promise, written in her own blood.

Like the Woodpecker Fairy, she entertained the prince, who returned her head, which reattached to her body, and at the end of three days he resumed his travels. When the hero and his horse had reached the boundaries of the Scorpion Witch's kingdom, they hurried on without resting till they came to a field covered with flowers, where reigned a perpetual spring. Every blossom was remarkably beautiful and filled with a sweet, intoxicating fragrance; a gentle breeze fanned them all.

So we have reached the place, master, said the horse, but we still have one great peril to face. A little further on is the palace where dwell Youth without Age and Life without Death. It is surrounded by a high, dense forest, where roam all the wild animals in the world, watching the gates day and night. They are very numerous, and it is almost beyond the bounds of possibility to get through the woods by fighting them; we must try, if we can, to jump over them. Buckle my girth as tight as you can, and when you have mounted, hold fast to my mane and press your feet close to my neck, that you may not hinder me.

The prince mounted, and in a moment they were close to the forest. The horse took a galloping start. As they flew upward, they glimpsed a palace that glittered so fiercely that it could not be looked upon, like the sun. They passed over the forest, and just as they were descending at the palace steps, one of the horse's hooves lightly touched the top of a tree, which awoke the whole woods. The wild animals howled so that the prince's hair stood on end. They circled him for the kill, but the mistress of the palace stopped them, sparing our hero's life out of pure pleasure, for she had never before seen a human being. Restraining the savage beasts, she soothed them, and sent them back to their haunts.

The mistress of the palace was a tall, slender, lovely lady, quite astonishing. When the young hero saw her, he stood still as though turned to stone. As she gazed at him she pitied him and said, Welcome, my handsome prince. What do you seek here?

I seek Youth without Age and Life without Death.

Then he dismounted from his horse and entered the palace, where he found another lady of the same age, as dazzling as the first one. The two sisters had a magnificent banquet served in golden dishes. They gave the horse liberty to graze wherever he chose, and afterward made him acquainted with all the wild beasts, so that he might rove about the forest in peace. The ladies entreated the prince to stay with them, saying that it was so tiresome to be alone. He did not wait to be asked a second time, but accepted the offer with the satisfaction of a man who had found precisely what he sought.

The prince spent a very long time at the palace without being aware of it, for he always remained just as young as he was when he arrived. He wandered about the woods, amused himself in the golden palace, lived in peace and quiet with the two ladies, enjoying their beauty and the beauty of the flowers, and the lightness of the sweet, pure air. His two wives let him do as he pleased, only entreating him not to enter one valley, which they called the Valley of Tears.

He often went hunting. But one day, while pursuing a hare, he shot two arrows without hitting the animal. Angrily chasing it, he discharged a third arrow, which struck it, but in his haste he had not noticed that he had passed through the Valley of Tears while following the game. He picked up his kill and turned toward home, but was suddenly gripped with a wrenching longing for his father and mother. He did not venture to speak of this wish to his consorts, yet by his grief and restlessness both sisters instantly perceived his condition. Oh luckless prince, you have passed through the Valley of Tears, they wailed in terror.

I did so, my dear ones, without meaning to be so imprudent, but now the longing to see my parents is killing me! Yet I cannot forsake you. I have already spent some days with you and have no cause to complain. So I'll go and see my parents once more, and then come back to you, never to leave you again.

Do not quit us, beloved prince! Your parents died two or three hundred years ago, and if you go, we fear you yourself will never return. Stay with us, for a presentiment of evil tells us that you will perish.

All the entreaties of the two ladies, as well as those of the horse, were unable to quiet the young hero's longing for his parents, which was fairly consuming him alive. At last the horse said: If you don't listen to me, master, whatever happens to you will be your own fault. I'll tell you something, and if you accept my condition, I'll take you back.

I'll accept it with many thanks, replied the prince. Let me hear it.

As soon as you reach your father's palace you will dismount, but I am to return alone in case you stay even an hour.

Be it so, the prince agreed.

They made their preparations for the journey. The prince embraced the ladies and bade them farewell. They sobbed and wept bitterly watching him ride away.

The prince and his faithful steed reached the country that had once been the kingdom of the Scorpion Witch, but they found cities there. The woods had become well-tilled fields. The prince questioned one person after another about the Scorpion Witch and her house. They answered that their grandfathers had heard from their great-great-grandfathers that such silly tales had once been told.

How is that possible? asked the prince. I came through this region myself only a short time ago.

The people laughed at him as if he were a lunatic or a person talking in his sleep, and the prince angrily rode on without noticing that his hair and beard were growing white. When he reached the realm of the Woodpecker Fairy, the same questions and answers were exchanged. The prince could not understand how these places had altered so much in so few days, and again he rode angrily on. He now had a white beard that reached his waist, and a tremor was creeping up from his feet through his legs.

Finally, the prince arrived at his father's empire. There he found new people, new towns, and everything so much changed that he could not recognize it. At last he came to the palace where he had been born. When he dismounted, the horse kissed his hand and said, I wish you good health, master. I'm going back to the place whence I came. If you want to go too, mount quickly, and we'll be off.

Farewell. I, too, hope to return soon.

The horse darted away with the speed of an arrow.

When the prince saw the ruined palace and the weeds growing around it, he sighed deeply and, with tears in his eyes, tried to remember how magnificent these places had once been. He walked around the building two or three times, recollecting how every room, every corner had looked. He found the remains of the stable where he had discovered the horse, and then went down into the cellar, whose entrance was choked up with rubble and crawling weeds. He groped along, holding up his eyelids with his hands, and scarcely able to stay standing, while his snowy beard now fell to his knees. He found nothing except a dilapidated old chest, which he opened. It seemed empty, but as he raised the lid a voice from the bottom said, Welcome. If you had kept me waiting much longer, I, too, should have gone to decay.

Then his Death, which had become completely shriveled in the chest, leapt out of its prison and seized him. The prince fell lifeless on the ground and instantly crumbled into dust.

Elena was wearing a one-piece swimsuit, which seemed unusual to Irina. It was navy with white polka dots and a lot of ruching down the sides. Maybe she was trying to imitate Irina's vintage pinup look. Or maybe there was something wrong. She hadn't gotten in the pool yet, when usually she was the first to leap in. She moved in a slow, hunched over way, as if she were in pain.

"Do you have cramps or something?" Irina asked. "I can get you painkillers."

"Cramps?"

"You know." Irina motioned to her lower abdomen.

"Yes, lady problems. No thank you. I will just warm myself here in the sun."

For a few minutes, they reclined with their eyes closed. Then Irina heard Elena's voice say, "I shave my toes now." It sounded curiously exhausted.

"What?"

"I was watching television the other day. There was a commercial on for a kind of wax for women. The commercial said the wax removed the unsightly hair from such places as your upper lip, bikini line, toes. Toes? I looked down at my feet. And there it was, unsightly hair on the top of the toes I had never before seen. I had been alerted of my deficiency. I could not unsee the little hairs."

"So now you shave them."

"Yes."

"I shave mine because the straps on high-heeled girly sandals will sometimes tug on them and it hurts."

They thoughtfully looked over each other's denuded toes. "I like your nail polish," Irina said.

"The color is called Femme Fatale," Elena answered flatly.

"That's more exciting than mine. Mine is called Cinnamon Spice."

These were the names a copywriter had given to a bright red and an orangey pink, trying to infuse these colors with sexy allure: a woman of lethal beauty and a spicy tang on the tongue.

"Really, they are just tiny pots of nasty-smelling paints," Elena said, as if she could hear what Irina was thinking.

"So you're not into pedicures, is what you're saying."

"Oh, I hate it when people touch my feet. I do it myself."

Irina pictured Elena crouched over her feet, gingerly painting the nude seashell pink of each of her toenails with a bitty paintbrush while wrinkling her nose at the chemical reek of the lacquer. "Why do you bother with it?" Irina asked.

"We have to, do we not?"

Irina hadn't thought about whether or not the ritual was compulsory. She just got weekly pedicures and manicures because it gave her something to do. But it was true, it must have been, in their position—they had to do it. Being young, pretty, and well-groomed was practically their vocation.

"I went to bed with Dragos," Irina blurted.

Elena sat up in her chaise longue. "What?"

"Dragos. Dragos fucked me."

"Ha! Did he drug you?"

"No."

Elena gazed pointedly at Irina, presumably reflecting on the fact that she had gone to bed with Dragos of her own volition, not under the influence of some kind of chemical. Was the act more or less shameful because she had chosen it? Sometimes Elena was as inscrutable as her husband. A less observant person than Irina might have ascribed their impassivity to their common Russianness, but that wasn't it. The textures of their silences were different. Elena had the sangfroid of someone who had had a lot of things done to her, Vasilii of someone who had done a lot of things to others.

"Interesting," Elena said. "Well, he has wanted you for a while."

"You knew this?"

Irina's tone sounded shocked enough to make Elena giggle. "It is hard not to. So, was he any good?"

Irina could not begin to explain to her friend what had happened when she went to bed with Dragos. It was entirely bizarre. The words *good* and *bad* seemed not to apply. Or if one of them did, then the other did too.

"What's *not* good, exactly, when it comes to sex?" Irina asked.

"If you do not know that, you are a fortunate girl." Elena gave a small, dry laugh. She, like Andrei, must have known what a bad fuck was. Worse, what if she didn't know what it was like when it was good? It was true that it was practically impossible for Irina to imagine Vasilii as a lover. Or stranger still—

"Were you with other men before Vasilii?"

Elena shrugged. "Some."

"Elena, how old were you for your first one?"

"However old a girl needs to be to be sold."

Irina went quiet. Did Elena mean that quite literally? Not just in the way a girl might give her body in the hopes of a marriage, but a real sale? Irina was about to ask if this happened through some kind of agency. And if that agency was the same kind that had made her matrimonial match with Vasilii. And if Vasilii somehow owned or operated this agency. And if Andrei was also involved somehow. If Andrei's traffic extended beyond luxury goods. Beyond counterfeit luxury goods. Beyond stolen cars. Beyond illegal drugs.

There was a great big ball in Irina's throat. There was so much crime so close by that she hardly had to reach out to touch it. But then again it was everywhere, even far, far away from the pleasures of Andrei's bed. You couldn't even buy a sack of oranges at the supermarket without exploiting somebody. You couldn't put clothes on your back to cover your nakedness without a pair of underpaid hands to sew them together for you. It was a stupid, losing gamble to try to be a good person in this world. The desert city had taught Irina about the house. The house—the house always wins.

"You know," Elena said, sighing and resting a limp hand on her sore belly, "maybe I want your painkillers after all. Do you have any good ones?"

0

The four ATMs are outside, around the corner of the building, two per wall. Behind them there is an ATM room accessed by upper and lower keys, where the bankers open up the backs of the machines to load them. To get to this room Irina and Amy have to walk across the bank floor with a big, unmarked bag filled with twenties. If somebody knew what to look for, knew when to tackle the bankers and run, it would be a fast and effective robbery. They move quickly. In the space of a deep inhale and exhale, they make it from the safety of behind the teller windows to the inside of the ATM room, locking the door behind them.

Each machine is named after a letter in the phonetic alphabet: Alpha, Bravo, Charlie, Delta. Alpha is the one with the sticky door; Irina has to give it a good yank to get it open. Then she pulls the metal shaft out of the machine's innards, where the money is packed.

"How many K we need in there?" Amy asks.

"Ten, I think."

Amy hands Irina the five packets of twenties one at a time. Irina lines them up in the long tray, one behind the other. When she breaks the Federal Reserve paper straps on them with a letter opener and pulls them out from the solid mass of cash, she does it with a peculiar violence that makes Amy ask her if she is okay.

"I can't believe I did this again!" Irina says, exasperated.

"Did what again?"

"Bad date last night."

"Was he a creep?"

"You could say that."

Irina pushes the metal shaft loaded with money back into the machine, hard, and then stands there without letting go of the handle. Yes, she's done it again. She had allowed a man to ruin her, as Andrei would have said, in microcosm over the course of one evening. Why did she let them do this to her?

Amy isn't saying anything, isn't moving. She is waiting for Irina to continue, so Irina does:

"I met a new man. It seemed to be going well; I liked his wit. Last night after dinner I went back with him to his place to watch a movie, a tragic war-torn love story. The kind of movie a man takes you to so that you'll cry and then he can comfort you. I was collaborating with his design, I was drinking his wine and we were getting pretty close on the couch, I was leaning on him. Except at the end when the titles were rolling he was the one who was crying. Tears pouring unchecked down his face without a sound. Made me wonder how long I was sitting there in the dark leaning against this weeping man. Made me feel sorry for him."

Irina shuts the back of Alpha and locks it. She opens Bravo.

"This one's almost empty. We're going to need a good twenty K in here."

"Here, let me load," Amy says gently, nudging Irina aside. Irina watches her tightly fit the neat packets of cash inside the long open tray, one at a time. When the money is all in, Irina reaches for the letter opener. "So, he was crying," she says, "and like an idiot I ask him with great care, 'What's the matter?' And he says, 'The lead actress looks so much like my ex.' And me, like an idiot, I'm full of drunk girl empathy, so I give him a hug. After a minute of me holding him he says, 'I'd rather not sleep alone tonight.' This is when it gets awkward."

The Federal Reserve straps on the cash packets make a satisfying crack as Irina breaks them with the letter opener. She pulls the straps out, leaving the money as one uninterrupted block, and drops them in the trash. "What would you have done?" she asks Amy.

"You mean would I have stayed?"

"Yes. When a crying man asks you to stay, what do you do?"

They are both standing there, while Amy is considering the question, when the silence is broken by a series of little electronic beeps in the machine from someone outside trying to use it.

"Out of fucking order, okay?" Irina shouts at the beeps through the metal guts of the machine, and the noises stop. She heaves a deep sigh. "Well, I stayed. I said, 'Okay, let's go to sleep, then.' I borrowed one of his T-shirts and got in bed with him. For a while we lay there and I watched car headlights from the street move across his wall. Then he caught me around the waist and pulled me in. When he went for a kiss I turned my face away and his tongue left a big wet streak down my cheek and I thought, This is my fault. Why am I here? Shrinking back from him as much as I could without fighting him, hoping he'd get the picture. He must not have cared too much about the picture because he pulled the T-shirt up and sucked on my tits so hard that it hurt and this is when I would have said no if I'd said it. But if I said no then he might really hurt me. So I let him. I let him and it didn't take long, he went to sleep right after. I was stuck there, in some residential neighborhood somewhere where there weren't buses at that hour and I was still too drunk to go anywhere anyway. So I would wait until the morning. You know what? I shouldn't have but I went to sleep. I went to sleep with this man in his bed and I woke up this morning with his arm around me. Can you believe that shit?"

"Whoa. Usually I'm the one cussing in here," Amy answers.

Irina slides the cash shaft back into place and closes the door on the back of the machine. "I slept with his arm around me," she says, her voice quieter this time.

"I'm sorry. It's okay. Sometimes that happens."

"Sometimes what happens?"

"Sometimes you're just tired."

Irina nods, her eyes far away. She turns the key to lock up Bravo and pulls it out. Her button-down shirt feels tight around her neck. Her pencil skirt feels tight around her hips. She hates her stupid banker clothes. Once again, she has let a man use her. Worse, she has unveiled her bleeding loneliness in a bank, at work, where she was supposed to be able to get away from herself. But Amy doesn't seem to mind. Amy picks up the bag of twenties and says, in the tender tone of a mother trying to make a hurt child forget a scrape, "Come on. Let's load Charlie."

Today, Irina stops in front of the empty house again on the way home. She looks it over to see if there are any further signs of degradation, if more of the paint has flaked off. If there are more cobwebs in the corners, if pieces of plaster have started to crumble from the walls. Maybe she didn't look closely enough last time, because as far as she can see nothing has changed. Except that today the door is closed. Whose hand might have shut it? Probably there was no hand. Just a passing breeze. When Irina nudges at the door with one finger, it does not give. She considers it for a few moments, considers turning on her heel and going home. Instead she roots around in her purse and takes out her bank employee identification card. She slides it carefully into the crack of the door. How embarrassing would it be for the card to break, half of her name remaining stuck in the side of the house as evidence of her wrongdoing?

Of course, nobody would care.

She works at the lock more or less randomly, not really expecting anything to happen. Her gesture is a lark; she is pretty certain that her lock picking is futile.

There is a click. The door yields and swings open a mere inch. Irina didn't know she was such an adept criminal. The men in her life must have rubbed off. Thinking of them gives her a moment's hesitation, but only a moment. She steps inside and waits for her eyes to adjust to the gloom.

In the kitchen, the dead refrigerator still gapes open, but the jar of green mayonnaise that was inside is gone. Its absence would be less odd if it looked as though the place had been cleaned since Irina was last here, but if anything, the layer of dust on the cheap Formica seems to be thicker.

She walks into the back of the house, farther than she went last time. There is a sliding door in the bedroom leading out to a deck, which itself has a few steps down into a scraggly backyard. Irina leans on the deck's railing, looking down at the sandy ground covered by a dried tangle of uninvited plants. She pictures herself back there tearing up weeds. Planting bulbs so that the next spring would be pink with flowers. Arranging a little table and chairs so she could sit out there with a glass of wine on breezy evenings and have the smell of blooms brush her face. Would a man live with her in the house? Yes. A man who loved her. But before she can even imagine the contented quiet of their undisturbed lives, at her feet materializes a child. A baby, crawling and gurgling happily. She picks up the baby. It laughs when she tickles its soft pudgy neck.

She does not know if the child is a boy or a girl. At that age, it hardly matters anyway. At that age, a person is only a pair of big eyes that know nothing yet. Only the insistent tugging of a mouth on a mother's breast, drawing sustenance from her body. This nonexistent child makes Irina's heart shrink into its shell like a snail poked with a stick. She recedes back into the bedroom, sliding the glass door shut after her. Through the emptiness of the kitchen, the living room, the entryway—where she will never hang her coat.

Out on the sidewalk, Irina pulls the front door closed after her with enough verve that it slams. She checks that it is locked. She walks away making sure not to look back at the empty house. Elena. How she envies Elena. It's odd to envy someone who is quite possibly dead. Still, Elena somehow had the backbone to ride away from the cataclysm. She'd decided to go and she went. Irina hadn't been woman enough for that. Irina had to be pushed out. She had to be exiled. She had to be cast out with no idea where she was going.

Irina feels cold to her bones. She knows she has to keep

moving or her frozen soul will never be found. She doesn't want to open her mind's eye, because the wind howling at her mind's ear and the cold flakes whipping at her mind's cheek tell her that all she will see is white. Snow. Snow. Snow as far as her heart can see.

Today Irina cannot shake the dim gaze of the security camera. It is as if the ceiling itself is looking at her, but there is no mind behind its eye to judge her. If she could sense judgment emanating from the white plaster, from the crown moldings, it might actually put her at ease. Instead the ceiling promises a whole lot of nothing. It will not point at her and roar. It will not cave in and engulf her in debris.

It feels so lonely, not being judged. It must have been why people made God.

Irina's fingers tap automatically on her computer's ten key, and the ceiling says nothing. She counts and counts and counts piles of meaningless money and the ceiling says nothing. It is all the more loathsome because there is nothing to loathe. Who watches the security camera footage anyway? Somewhere there is a luminescent checkerboard of screens playing to an empty room in mute shades of gray.

A man comes to Irina's window to cash a check. He presents identification. He endorses the check in front of her. She inspects his signature against the identification.

"Twenties okay?" she asks.

The man nods. The amount on the check is $238.72. She pulls bills out of her cash drawer and counts for him:

"Twenty, forty, sixty, eighty, one hundred." In a neat fan of five bills.

"Twenty, forty, sixty, eighty, two hundred." In a neat fan of five bills overlaid on the first fan.

"Twenty, thirty, thirty-five, thirty-six, thirty-seven, thirty-eight." In a neat fan of six bills overlaid on the other two.

"And sixty-two cents," she says, dropping the change directly into his palm. Two quarters, a dime, two pennies. He pockets the change while she closes the fans of money and makes a neat stack of bills to hand over. He does not feel compelled to re-count them before shoving them in his wallet.

"Thank you. Have a good day," Irina recites. The man grunts something like assent and leaves.

When the glass door swings shut after him, Irina looks up at the singular eye in the ceiling and asks it mutely, *Did you see?*

No reply is forthcoming, of course. No policeman bursting in to bend her over the counter and roughly cuff her. No thundering voice admonishing her from a hidden speaker. No accountability whatsoever. And yet. And yet here she has purposefully shortchanged a man by a dime, right here. Right here under the eye of the security camera.

She doesn't even check to see if somebody is watching when she picks a dime out of her change till and, without taking her eyes from the ceiling's gaze, puts it slowly, almost theatrically, in her pocket. Her eyes say, *Come get me*.

She wants to be gotten and no one will get her. No one will come collect all her debts. If she wanted, she could walk along the metal wall to the vault and find the palindrome number 21012. She could open the safe-deposit box she has stolen the key for and steal whatever is in the box too; it would make no difference. That it would make no difference is perhaps the reason why she has not done it yet. She would not be able to withstand more indifference from the universe.

On one of the one-dollar bills she has given the man who cashed his check, on the bill of smallest value, Irina has written in a loose, careless scrawl, slanted with speed, without lifting her pen between words so that the entire phrase is one loopy line, its words separated by only a flat line: *youth without age and life without death.*

Something was different that month. The fatigue was the same as usual: it felt almost drugged, filling her with a warm lust for sleep. It sunk her into a sensuous bliss when she curled up in bed, gathering the plush comforter around her drowsy body. The hunger was what was not the same as usual. Usually she craved the greasy and the savory. Hot French fries with too much salt on them, the grains smarting her taste buds. A juicy cheeseburger with a layer of crisp bacon, the hot blood in the meat flooding her mouth when she bit down. A wedge of steaming pizza, with bright, salty red rounds of pepperoni crumbling into the gooey cheese when she chewed down a too big mouthful. All the best, most American foods. But this month was different: her body wanted the sweet and the soft. A brioche smothered in honey, the bread so yielding it could be wrenched apart by the tongue. A cut mango, the fruit's mellow flesh melting into liquid gold once bitten. Angel food cake washed down with a mug of hot milk, combining in her mouth to taste like the soft, warm version of the color white. She wanted the texture as much as the taste of these tender things, an approximation of some smooth ambrosia she'd eaten only in dreams. Forgotten mother's milk.

What if this month the blood didn't come? She wasn't late yet, but her own body seemed to be turning foreign on her. Her urine smelled strange. All smells, actually, were a bit off and more intense.

If this were really happening, she would not know for another week at least. Even a pregnancy test would not tell her yet. It was ridiculous of her to think she could feel it this early. If there was indeed an incipient life inside her, it was not even the size of a poppy seed. Even the princess with her famous pea would not be able to feel something so small. It would be less than a disturbance, less than a grain of sand on the beach, less than a fleeting thought.

Even when the seed took, many times the body flushed it out before a woman knew she was pregnant. If the seed had indeed taken, whose was it?

It must have been that she was just trying to thrill herself, scare herself. It was her idle, corrupt life that was doing it to her. It made her thirst for a sign. It made her look up at the sky waiting for a retribution that would not come. It was the men who were doing this to her, swallowing her into the underworld, and finally a tiny part of her was fighting the descent. She needed to talk to a woman. There was only one she could call.

Andrei's father had gone to another village by the time Andrei's mother knew she was pregnant. Andrei's mother gave a few coins to some other Gypsy to track him down and tell him of the impending arrival. When Irina asked Andrei what had happened after that, Andrei shrugged and said, "There's nothing to tell." He must have meant to let her think that the Gypsy had pocketed the money and didn't go to look for his father. Or that the Gypsy had delivered the message but that it was not heeded—for how does a moment of careless abandon become a person? It was the woman's body that willed a person into being, a woman's body that ran its blood through the moment of careless abandon until a child was formed. What had the man's body done except indulge in brief forgetfulness? A man was essentially a bystander. Did it really matter which man a child came from after all?

But what if it had been worse? What if Andrei's father had gotten the message and come back? What if he'd asked the woman to come with him in his Gypsy wagon and she'd said no? What if he'd tried to live in her family's house, giving up his nomad ways and submitting to the hateful stares of her parents, to do right by his accidental creation? What if he'd tried and he simply couldn't stand it and left again? What if he had met Andrei, held Andrei as a blurry-eyed baby, felt the grip of the child's tiny hand on his index finger while his heart swelled with recognition? What if he'd done all that and still gone away? Andrei seldom got genuinely angry, angry in a way that was not tinged with irony, but Irina had a feeling that if she asked about such things, he might be devoid of quips. He would turn quiet and become cold, a cold that was a greater augur of violence than the hot flare of his heedless temper. Andrei had only one father, and that father was absent, and that was that. He did not want to talk about fathers and fathering; the whole question was one that did not deserve to be addressed.

For Irina, it was clearly different. She had two fathers, who somehow both had the qualities of phantoms. There was the father who sent for her. Granted, he did so partially at the insistence of his wife. Still, this father wanted her; he waited for her; he gave her a room in his house. He taught her to speak; he forged her mind; he made her an American. And yet there was a strange remoteness in him, something not quite right. An uncharitable soul might have surmised that there was an ineffable emptiness at his center—but Irina didn't want to be an uncharitable soul. Perhaps the fault was hers. Perhaps it was she who was remote. Perhaps they were both inept, reaching for each other in all the wrong ways. Were they both haunted by the first father? The father who sent her away, or worse, did not even know she ever existed? That father gave her no sustenance, taught her nothing, gave her nothing but life. That father had nothing to do with the forging of her mind—he hadn't been there to make her a Romanian.

Somehow these two fathers had brought her to Andrei's bed. Somehow these two had made Andrei a father himself. Somehow Irina would have to tell him.

Whatever happened, whether a child was born or not, it was too late. Their union had made a ghost that would follow Irina around forever. That ghost must have been a certainty from the moment she had chosen to get in Andrei's car on that hot summer day before she was legally a grown woman.

The ghost would forever wander the world unseen, wearing Irina's face. Somewhere, a woman with a name but no body was wearing a string of large, blushing pearls, matching earrings, a lavender sapphire on her right hand, and a ruby on her left—like a woman betrothed on both sides. She had never been given life, but there she was. Her name was Vasilica Andreescu and she was a series of numbers in a bank database. For someone who did not exist, she certainly had a lot of money. She was lucky not to exist. She would never have to be anyone's mother.

How late are you?" Elena asked.

"Only a couple of days. It's not so much that; it's more that I feel strange," Irina answered.

Elena looked her up and down. "You seem good to me."

"It's not that I feel bad—just odd. Do you have the test?"

Elena took out a rectangular cardboard box from her crinkly grocery bag. The box was a saturated pink, almost magenta. *FREE PREGNANCY TEST,* the box announced. It had been a two-for-one promotion.

"Why would you need an extra?" Irina asked. Elena shrugged. Irina tore open the box and took out one of the packets inside. It looked like a long candy, wrapped in plastic the same loud color as the box. Inside was a white plastic stick with a little window to view the results. It had a cotton tip with a translucent protective cover on it.

"So I'm supposed to pee on this," Irina said flatly, turning the plastic stick in her hands.

"You are not vomiting?" Elena asked.

"No, not yet. If anything I'm really hungry all the time."

"Well, you could just be hungry."

"Just...just stay while I take the test, will you?"

Elena sat on the bed while Irina went into the bathroom. It was some minutes before she came back out, her clothes askew, looking as disheveled as if she'd been in a fight.

"So?" Elena asked.

"We have to wait a little bit now. Three minutes." Irina plopped down heavily next to her friend. She sighed. "It's probably nothing. I'm probably just freaking out."

"If it is a child, it is Andrei's, yes?"

Irina would have liked to be able to be outraged at such a question. She had tried her best not to consider the paternity possibilities too deeply. The fact was that the timing of this new development was terrible, that this had to have happened the month she'd gone to bed with Dragos. There was a chance, however slim, that it was his seed that had done it. Irina tried to answer Elena, but nothing came out. She only felt the blood drain from her face, leaving her cold.

"Irina." Elena spoke softly, with a slight edge that might have been reproach.

"He practically sent me there!" Irina snapped. "It wasn't even my idea!"

A silence. Elena put her hand on Irina's arm. They looked at each other. Elena's eyes seemed even bluer than usual, as if her feelings were saturating the color.

"Look," she said, attempting calm Russian pragmatism, "we will do what has to be done if it comes to that. Nobody is going to die."

Irina did not even have to ask Elena whether she was sure

that no one would die before the pronouncement collapsed under the weight of doubt. Given the men they were dealing with, maybe somebody would, and soon.

"It's true," Elena whispered. "If what is happening to you happened to me and I carried the child of some other man Vasilii made me go to bed with, he would do only one of two things. He would marry me or he would kill me."

"You think Andrei might marry me?" Irina's voice squeaked.

"Andrei is not Vasilii." Elena waved her hand dismissively. "Andrei would not kill you."

The two girls did not notice that Irina had asked a question about a marriage and Elena had answered a question about an execution.

"Come on. It's been three minutes," Irina said.

In the yellow light of the bathroom, the two girls' heads met over the tiny window in the white plastic stick.

"Two lines." Elena breathed out.

The lines were the same glaring pink as the box the stick had come in. The line on the right looked slightly lighter than the one on the left but was indisputably there.

"One line says not pregnant. Two lines says pregnant," Irina announced, reading from the folded flier that came in the box, as if she needed to. As if saying this aloud as calmly as possible would make it so she was not watching her own body from a great height.

"We should do it again to make sure," Elena said, catching her friend by the arm and steadying her.

Irina laughed. "There. Now I know. That's why it was two-for-one. That's why they put an extra test in the box. For when the results are positive and you can't fucking believe it and you have to do it again and hope that your fucked-up life might reverse itself. Elena, I can't do it again right now. I'm all out of pee."

Without answering, Elena gently guided Irina out of the bathroom, across the bedroom and living room, and into the kitchen. She started to open cabinets.

"What are you looking for, Elena?"

"Something to drink. We have to make you make more pee."

"It's that cabinet there. I don't think there's anything to drink in there besides vodka and wine. You want vodka or wine? Or vodka in some wine?"

Elena wrinkled her nose and shook her head. "Tired of it," she said.

"Me too."

Besides, if Irina was really with child, shouldn't she give up drink? Isn't that what they said all good expectant mothers were supposed to do? What a ludicrous idea. Irina, a mother. She had not yet felt any nausea, but at that moment, the need to vomit rushed up her body from the soles of her feet to the crown of her head—and then went away as quickly as it came.

"Look." Elena reached into the back of the cupboard and pulled out a half-empty bottle of something viscous and bright. Fuchsia, almost the same color as the lines on the test. "Grenadine, like when we were children!"

"I didn't even know we had that in there. It must be for mixed drinks? I don't get it. I've never seen Andrei have a mixed drink in my life."

Elena put some of the syrup in two glasses and then filled them up with water from the tap.

"America calls this a Shirley Temple," Irina observed when her friend handed her the concoction.

"Who is Shirley Temple?"

"She was a kid actress many years ago, in the thirties, I think. She had cute corkscrew curls in ribbons and sang songs about lollipops and things."

"And now," Elena observed, "she is probably dead."

"Not yet. I think she's in politics or something."

Both girls took a first sip. The drink was intensely sweet and did indeed taste like more innocent times.

"Politics?" Elena said. "Americans are strange." She was about to giggle at the incongruous idea of a child actress turned politician when she flinched slightly, put her glass down.

"Are you okay?"

"Fine, fine." Elena waved her hand as if to sweep some feelings away. "You drink all of that down. You drink all of that down and make more pee."

The second time, Irina did not come back out to talk to Elena before the test yielded its result. She stayed in the bathroom with it for the interminable three minutes, the door locked behind her, watching the two lines appear slowly in the little results window as if she could will them not to by concentrating hard enough. The lines came ever so lightly at first and then deepened, more sure of themselves, until the answer was definite. The oracle had spoken. Irina was expecting. She tossed the stick into the trash can and put her face in her hands. She breathed deeply for a few moments, smelling the sweat on her palms. Then she opened the door.

"So?" Elena said.

"Yes."

"It's really real then."

"Yes."

The two of them stood in the doorway as if in the wake of an earthquake, looking around at a shaken world. What to do now? Had the test been negative, there would have been more waiting, and then probably relief. But now there could be no more waiting. Someone had to be told. Unless the incipient person inside her suddenly thought better of coming into this broken world under such unhinged circumstances and decided it would be best to recede back into oblivion. But was a merciful miscarriage what Irina really wanted? Rationally, it ought to have been—but she simply could not resist the beginning of another story. Even if the bitty thing inside her was nothing but a blank page, a blank page demanded words, demanded to be written, as harrowing as the story might turn out to be. To tear up the blank page and disperse its white flakes to the four winds was awful, more awful than any cataclysm. Oblivion was worse than any hell. And so, it was hell that Irina now wanted. It was hell she had brought upon herself.

Why did it feel as though this had to happen? Why did it feel as though some part of her had willed it?

Without a word, Elena went to Irina and hugged her. The two girls held each other tightly for what felt like a long time, swaying gently. Irina smelled the light fragrance Elena had sprinkled on her shoulders to make herself appealing to Vasilii. The two girls had picked it out together in a store the previous week. The previous week felt so far away! Hot tears welled inside Irina and began to gush out of her eyes. When Elena felt the wetness on her neck, she cooed something unintelligible that sounded like a comfort. Something in Russian that her mother must have spoken to soothe her when she was a little girl and hurt herself. Irina was about to ask what the words meant when Elena quaked in Irina's arms, made a noise that sounded like a sob. Was she crying too?

Elena crumpled away from Irina's embrace. She was suddenly doubled over on the bed. She was not crying. She was in some other kind of pain. She was breathing fast, her eyes wide and afraid.

"Elena." Irina gasped. "You're bleeding."

Elena looked down at herself. There was a small red stain on her belly, spreading on the light blue silk blouse with lace embellishments that the two girls had also picked out together, in a store with piano music and the clothes neatly spaced out on the racks, some expensive store that was receding rapidly into another life.

Elena covered the stain with her hand. She would not look her friend in the face when asked what was the matter, what was happening.

"Do you have a cut there? It looks like a cut," Irina said. At these words, Elena looked plainly terrified.

"Please, let me see."

"No."

"Let me see!"

Elena shook her head but without conviction. Irina pulled her friend's hand off her belly. "Let me see," she whispered, unbuttoning her friend's shirt. There were Elena's small pert breasts, encased in the pretty lingerie Irina had prescribed for her. Under the bra's cradle was where sanity stopped. If Irina had been the kind of person who shrieked when confronted with horror, she would have. But she merely stared in the deafened silence that follows an explosion, while her heart thrummed thunderously in her ears.

A careful hand had written on Elena's belly in small, tidy letters Irina could not read. There were many words etched into the skin with something thin and clearly very sharp, from her diaphragm down, disappearing into the waistband of her skirt. The wounds looked nearly fresh. The alphabet was Cyrillic. One of the words, near the belly button, had been rubbed raw and was bleeding. That was the word that had soaked through Elena's shirt.

"What is this? Who did this to you? Did Vasilii do this to you?" Irina demanded.

"With a tiny knife," Elena said, finally looking into Irina's face. "One of those tiny knives doctors use for surgery."

A scalpel. That was the word she was looking for. Both girls were pale, stunned. One at what she was seeing, the other at being discovered. What had been seen could not be unseen. What had been seen turned Elena's eyes the bluest, most furious blue they had ever been. A blue like a flying shard of ice in a snowstorm. There was no going back to the way things were.

"That fucker!" Irina spat. "That fucking fucker!"

Yes, so many things had happened and something had to be done. They had all accrued too many debts. They were all too far in the red.

Trei

This image here is a royal seal for a medieval voivode who bore the same name as the last man Romania ever called voivode. It is round, like a coin. At its summit, between the sun and the moon, flies an eagle with a cross in its beak. This is the coat of arms of the principality of Wallachia. Below this is a shield bearing the head of an aurochs, crowned by a star. This is the coat of arms of the principality of Moldavia. Below this are two standing lions gripping a sword, treading on seven mountains. This is the coat of arms of the principality of Transylvania. Bracketing the three symbols are two crowned figures. Who is this voivode who ruled all three principalities hundreds of years before they would come together as Romania?

Along the circular edge of the seal is written in Cyrillic Old Church Slavonic, *Io Michael Voivode of the Lands Wallachia Transylvania Moldavia through the very Grace of God*.

The voivode on the seal held these three lands together for a solitary summer in the year 1600. He was assassinated the following year by a former ally. A twentieth-century scholar was known to have observed that never in Romanian history was such glory so closely followed by such failure. Nineteenth-century unifiers were known to have cited Michael the Brave as their precursor. It is not known whether the voivode Michael had in mind any such nation. It is known that he was greatly ambitious, an exceptional personality. His rule was war-filled.

A stern bearded face. A voluminous hat. Those are sustained in representations of him. However, the features of the face change shape; his gaze shifts from straight on to sideways and back again in various portraits of him. He is praised as a great Turk killer, a force against the oppressor. Unless he is himself an oppressor. Sometimes it takes a bit of work to piece together whose neck is under the boot, and what's more, it is not certain who is wearing the boot. Somebody must be. There are a lot of crushed necks.

Like all Romanian voivodes under Ottoman rule, he had to purchase his throne with heavy bribes and then pay extortionate tributes to the Porte. For this the prince placed a heavy tax burden on the peasantry, and carried much debt with Ottoman creditors. The story about Michael states that this arrangement did not suit him. The story states that he summoned all his creditors to his palace to divide some of the money owed among them. There would be a great feast in a wooden hall in which the gold would be dispensed. It was a foggy late afternoon when the delegates arrived, the growing crepuscular dark aiding the mist in shrouding everything so that one unfamiliar with the landscape could not be quite certain of the shape of things. The voivode Michael himself was waiting to honor them; he was easy to recognize by the large bulbous fur hat on which bobbed a great plume. Draped over him was a ponderous cape of a red so saturated that it left no doubt that massive quantities of expensive dye were used to achieve the color. This made a good impression of the delegates: it spoke of the wealth he'd accumulated, guaranteeing the large payment he would imminently bestow upon them. With interest.

Known for being acerbic and terse, Michael was with them conciliatory and flower-tongued. We have set a great hall for you, he told them. It is across the courtyard. Enter first, will you please, as my welcomed guests of honor.

There was indeed an appealing scent of cookery, which the delegates followed through a door into a large, dim space. One looked up into the wooden latticework under the roof and thought, These Wallachians are truly backward—their grand hall looks no better constructed than a barn. Another looked down and saw the dirt floor. Another looked around and saw the immense hollowness of the place. There was only a pit inside, over which roasted a solitary pig, impaled from mouth to fundament, its face still reading an expression of startlement. The spit had not been turned in a while; the soft flesh of the pig's underside was starting to char, tinting the good meat smell with the tang of something burned. There was another smell too, underpinning the others, as if something had been soaked into the straw stuffed in the dank corners of the edifice. Only one of the delegates had time to whirl around on his boot heel before the door was slammed shut behind them with a thunderous clap. He threw himself against the entrance as fast as he could but it would not budge—already bolted.

Another delegate took a step backward farther into the darkness and disturbed something leafy with his foot. The voivode Michael's voice came through the wall, as intimate as if he were standing right among them, his announcement carried on breath instead of shivering through the wood. Your tribute, my lords, the voice said, and then somehow found the self-restraint not to laugh despite its evident glee. It might have been that Michael was listening for their reaction.

It was then that the delegates saw that the leafy things were records documenting all the loans they had given the voivode, neatly stacked. The parchment had on them the same smell that emanated from the sprawling straw. The Turks had been locked in the barn with their own accounting. Outside, Michael's voice barked an order in a language they did not understand. One of the delegates screamed. Howled, even, like a cornered wolf. It did not take long for the great heat to surround them close as the devil's breath, the fire licking away at the walls. Their eyes stung with smoke. The flames exploded into a true blaze when they touched the straw, whatever was soaked into it making the conflagration bloom forth into a great yellow plume. One of the delegates violently shoved the accounting documents away with his foot when he realized that they, like all things permeable in this death trap, had been splashed in something that made the fire burn hotter and faster.

It was no use kicking up the papers, snared as they were. But the pages were beautiful as they caught flame while they flew up, up, up farther into the eaves, the voivode's debt tremblingly devoured by heat and light.

Irina, what do you think I can do about it? Do you think I can go to the police?"

"We have to do something! We can't just let him go on cutting her like that."

"Look, it is very sad, but there is nothing we can do about it."

"You need to talk to Vasilii. If you don't talk to him, I will."

Andrei gave Irina a long, hard look. She would not avert her furious eyes from his. "I would strongly advise you not to do that," he said evenly.

"You are a maggot." Irina's voice turned strident.

Andrei did not respond.

"A cringing coward," Irina went on.

"Look, he is not going to kill her. If he was going to do that, he would have done it by now. And he is not going to cut her up where anyone can see, a pretty girl like that. He has no use for a maimed wife."

Irina could not remember the last time she felt this angry. And yet she was totally impotent. Her powerlessness only stoked her rage. As Andrei's little woman, she was a subordinate's subordinate, a position that had seldom bothered her before. It was usually rather pleasant to be beneath notice. But when something needed to be done, the freedom of not mattering closed its metal teeth on her and turned into a prison.

Andrei was staring at Irina curiously. "So," he said, "what was the other thing?"

"The other thing?"

"You said you had two things to talk to me about. If the first thing was about Vasilii carving obscenities into his young bride with a razor, what could the second thing possibly be? What follows that?"

"A scalpel. She said it was a scalpel. And I don't know that they were obscenities. They were in Russian."

"Darling, I'm making the rather simple assumption that anything written into the flesh of a young girl with a blade is bound to be obscene, even if it's Bible verses. You cannot argue against that, no?"

Indeed she could not. It was difficult for her to speak today. Her dissent was inchoate, and would go unheeded anyway.

"They called him the butcher scribe, in the Soviet Army," Andrei said to fill the silence, with a certain wonder. "He was a master of the question. He could make anyone admit anything with no props whatsoever. No cattle prod to the anus, no pretend executions, no bucket drownings. With just the words from his clever mouth and his two hands, he could make any prisoner sing whatever was requested. He made up the lyrics and they sang. They said he enjoyed wielding a blade. Nothing big, something small like a razor. It was enough. He was like an alpinist who could reach the summit of a mountain with nearly no equipment. Just a rope and some crampons. An artist."

"What? You mean he's trying to get some kind of information out of Elena?"

"Oh no, I don't think so. He probably does it for old time's sake. To relive his youth and all that. Why else would he order a girl all the way from home when he could get one here with all his money? He could cut up an American if he wanted. If he paid her enough."

Did Andrei really not feel anything for Elena? Was he really that comfortable with the sick ways of this shit world? Could she really love such a man? His callousness had to be a shield. It had to be. His irony, his detachment, his seamy jokes—they were all to hide something soft or else she could not love him.

Or maybe it was just the taste of his body she loved so much.

"The other thing, Irina. Go on. You did not have that urgent look on your face just for your sliced-up little Russian friend. Tell me the other thing—you would rather not be put to the question, would you?"

The question. It was such a delicate way to refer to torture. As if there were only one question.

Irina felt as if she were standing at a windy cliff edge, getting up the courage to leap over the side, into a churning pool of ice-cold water. She didn't know the depth of this pool. It would, at best, shock her body into breathlessness. It might be shallow, the rocks just below the surface, waiting to dash her bones to jagged fragments. Little fishes would peck bits of brain from her shattered skull. She would dissolve into the blind sea.

"Andrei," she said, "I'm pretty sure I'm pregnant."

It was Andrei's turn to have nothing to say. His eyes widened. He didn't need to ask her to repeat herself. For a moment he looked downright scared. It was an expression so unusual for his face that it made Irina want to reach out and hold his trembling hand.

"No." He exhaled weakly, as if the word had been punched out of him.

Irina went to soothe him but he subtracted himself from her touch like a wounded animal. He left the room quickly, as if afraid her affection might burn him. She didn't know whether to go after him. She didn't know whether to comfort him or seek his comfort—or if it was better to let his body do whatever it needed to do.

It took him less than a minute to come back. When he entered the room, his stride was calm and decisive. But his face was distorted. There was something wrenched about the mouth, a metal glint in the eyes. In his right hand he carried the pistol from his desk drawer. In his left hand he clenched three bullets, their smooth dull brass warming up in his sweaty palm. Without looking at Irina, he opened the gun's chamber with a flick of his wrist and loaded in the bullets: "One for you," he said, "one for Dragos, and maybe, if I deem it necessary after, one in reserve for me."

He aimed the gun—not at her face or her heart, but at her womb. Irina felt the cold from his eyes penetrate her very flesh, course its way around her body like blood. The edges of her vision were starting to blur with white, as if snow were trying to eat her sight.

"You're not serious," she said, in a voice she attempted to keep steady.

"I am not serious," he repeated, dryly, as if considering the idea that he was joking and dismissing it.

"Andrei, I love you," she said, pleading.

"You little whore, I love you too, too much. What a disaster, darling. What a fucking disaster."

He lowered the gun. With great care, he put it down on the couch pillow, as if it were delicate and needed a rest. Then he sat heavily and suddenly on the couch next to his downed weapon, as if someone had kicked the backs of his knees. "What you are is my fault," he said, the chill draining from his eyes.

Irina put her trembling hand on her belly. She was mother to whatever was in there, fed by her own blood.

"The baby is yours, Andrei. It doesn't belong to Dragos."

It was the first time Irina had called the thing inside her a baby. The word clearly hit Andrei hard too; he had tears in his eyes when he answered, "I know it could not possibly be mine."

"How many times was I with you? I was with Dragos for one afternoon. It has to be yours."

"Irina, in all my life I have never made a woman pregnant. And Dragos—Dragos might be twice as rich if he hadn't had to pay for all the abortions of his pillhead lady friends. The timing is just too damned convenient, darling, isn't it?"

"Even if it's not yours, it's yours. As I am yours."

Irina watched Andrei trying to swallow down the idea that he had made life. She knew how he felt. She still could not wrap her mind around the fact that she had made life herself. For a man, it was easier to turn the idea away, to say, *That thing is not mine*. For a woman, there was no escape.

Andrei opened his arms to Irina, but for a moment she did

not obey the summons. She could still see the revolver sitting quietly among the pillows. Then something broke in her and she went to him. She went to him and let him enfold her, breathing in the warm scent of his neck, which she loved so much. She felt his body tremble like a fallen leaf in the wind. There was a ragged gasp. Was it a sob? Was he crying?

"What are we to do?" he said. "Are we to marry? To make a little American family? That is more than crazy for us."

She looked up at him, at his swollen red lips and his wet, gleaming eyes, and could not imagine how to answer such a proposal, if what he'd said had been a proposal. He must have seen the questioning terror in her eyes because he smiled and said, without the rising inflection of a question, "How do you stand me, my darling. How can you possibly stand me."

It was decided that Elena would be the one to accompany Irina to the abortion clinic. This was a hushed business better suited to females, a business with no fathers. Irina had considered being angry that Andrei would not be there, but then there was no point in it.

It was Vasilii who answered the door when Irina knocked.

"She will be out shortly," he said. "Would you like a vodka?"

Irina shook her head.

"Are you sure?" he said. "You might want to dull the poor thing's senses before you scrape it out of you."

Irina gave him a savage look. She could not remember ever having been alone with Vasilii. Now was the time to say something to him, to admonish and shame him. At least let him know that she knew about him, let him know that he wasn't getting away clean. She opened her mouth to start in on him but found that she hadn't any words. He had a vaguely benevolent, expectant look on his face. He was humoring her anger.

"They called you the butcher scribe," she finally said, in a strangely matter-of-fact tone.

"They did," he answered. "They called me the surgeon scribe at first, because of the precision of my cuts. When I heard the nickname, it made me laugh. I told them that they must not call me that, because a surgeon cuts people to heal them. That is not why I cut people. So I told them, Call me the butcher scribe if you must indulge in these sorts of schoolyard monikers."

How could Irina possibly hope to rattle a man like that? He was as calm as a blanket of snow on a sleeping wasteland, after the storm had abated. What manner of monsters were hibernating in the frozen ground Irina could only imagine.

Elena emerged to greet her, in a drapey frock the same shade of pink as the one she had been married in. She was all wide eyes and delicate bones. When she saw her husband and her friend standing there together, she gave them both a tentative smile.

"Onwards, then," Vasilii announced with equanimity, scooting the two girls out the door as if he were a father sending two children to the park to play to get them out of his hair.

It was a beautiful clear day with no distinct temperature. In the car, Elena did not have to turn on either the cooling or the warming system.

"I didn't know you could drive," Irina commented, watching her friend as she pulled out of the driveway with what looked like a hint of trepidation.

"Vasilii taught me."

"Oh? How was that?"

"He was nice. Fatherly and gentle."

Was Elena being deeply, profoundly sarcastic? It was true that Irina had never heard the man raise his voice. Plus she had just seen that strange, calm fatherliness in him when he sent them out the door. That equanimity was what allowed him his casual brutality. His horrid gift was the ability to hold gentleness and murder so close together. Andrei at least kept the two extremes apart with a thick wall of irony.

"I don't have a license, of course," Elena felt compelled to clarify.

"Elena," Irina said sternly. "Elena, this is insane. You have to leave."

"No."

"You can't stay with a husband who cuts you up for fun. He's going to kill you."

"No."

What had she said no to the second time? Her not staying or him killing her?

"What is he writing on you anyway?"

Elena shook her head vehemently, trying her best to keep her moistening eyes on the midafternoon traffic. She was not going to talk about this—whatever this blood text on her body was.

"If it's because you don't have money, I have a little of my own that Andrei doesn't keep track of. I can give you enough for a plane ticket. Go home to your mother—please."

"My mother would send me back."

"Then—then go wherever the fuck! The Bahamas. The Maldives. Brazil. Wherever people like us go when they're trying to save themselves. Save yourself—please. For my sake if nothing else."

Elena heaved a deep sigh. She quickly wiped at her cheek. Irina did not even see the stray tear. "It cannot be that easy," Elena said.

"Look, it is! Just get out."

"Vasilii would find me, and then he would kill me for certain. And then he would kill my whole family. Why do you think my mother would send me back here? Irina. Don't be so…"

Elena's admonition was left hanging there. Irina could not believe her friend was somehow in the thick of a situation that was even worse and more urgent than the one she was in, which would be resolved within the hour.

"So you're going to stay and take it when you really should leave," Irina said angrily.

The two girls looked at each other. It was no use being mad at the one getting slashed up but Irina had to be mad at something. She hated the whole world that was doing this to them.

It was then that Elena said something that Irina should have paid attention to. She said, "Not yet."

Irina did not answer, possibly did not even hear, because they had arrived in front of the clinic, a squat gray building that looked like a suburban middle school. Elena killed the engine. For a minute, neither of them moved, looking straight ahead through the windshield at the innocuous-looking place where they snuffed incipient lives in order to avoid ruining lives in progress. "How do you feel…about *it?*" Elena asked, motioning to her lower abdomen.

"I know it's stupid, but I wish that—I wish that I didn't have to."

"Oh. I know."

The sadness in the car was like a mist that was swallowing them both, making them shivery and foggy-eyed. What did Elena know? Had she done this before? As if to answer the unspoken query, Elena said, "Don't worry. It won't hurt too much. They are putting you out."

After making this pronouncement, she unhooked her seat belt, letting it snake over her body and tautly put itself away. Irina undid hers also. “Elena,” she asked softly. “Did you…did you have this done?”

What she really wanted to ask was whether Elena had to have this done without being put out. Did she feel the scraping? Did she—did she see what it looked like, the tiny red thing they carved from the center of her?

Elena took Irina’s hand. “You must give yourself all the time you need, to mourn,” she said gently. “Even if they tell you it was nothing, it was not a person, and that you are being a foolish girl. They do not know. Remember all you must, because if you try to forget it gets even worse.”

Irina didn’t have to ask what that meant. She already knew that oftentimes buried things would not stay buried. They clawed their way back up from the ground to roar hidden crimes at the world and collapse lives. That was the truest form of justice: up from the inside. Not from the outside. The outside turned the same glazed, blind eye toward the innocent and the corrupt.

It would be chilly inside the clinic, from the unnecessary air-conditioning. Elena would have to go back out to the car to fetch Irina her sweater. Neither of them would have the heart to look over the old magazines in the waiting room. They would sit together in utter silence until Irina’s name was called, and when the call came Elena would squeeze Irina’s hand one last time. Then, in the operating room, there would be the moment when Irina would begin to count backward in a language she was supposed to have forgotten. But this moment was in the future. For now they were still in the car. For now, presumably, they could still turn back, even though they both knew they would not.

"What do they do with the little ones, after?" Elena asked.

Little ones was a strange thing to call them, possibly even worse than calling them babies.

"I think they burn them," Irina answered.

"Ah. Better than throwing them in the trash," Elena said placidly, then: "Maybe we are breathing them in, right now."

What a thought. A tiny holocaust of things that were not yet lives being exhaled into the very atmosphere.

And yet is all the particulate matter hanging in the air not made of the dead? Do we not take disintegrated leaves, decomposed corpses, torched palaces, forgotten dreams into our bodies with every breath?

That day was the last time Irina saw Elena. That day when they drove to the innocuous-looking clinic to cleanse Irina of new life. Of course, there was no doubt that this was the right decision. For Irina to bring a child into her situation would have been an act of suicide. She could not have chosen a man more wrong than Andrei to be her child's father. The very wrongness of him made her sure he was somehow fated. Why did she think like this? Surely reasonable people did not think like this. And she—she who was supposed to be so intelligent. At least, a variety of tests at school had told her so. But even she knew that *intelligent* and *reasonable* did not mean the same thing. *Intelligent* did not even mean *sane*.

Why are people so driven toward the chance to make new life when they will inevitably bungle it with the same stupidities that ruined their own lives? Every time it is the same walking disaster. The child will turn out a whore or a criminal just like the rest of them. There was Irina, for example. She had been given every advantage, been shoved into the mold of a young American with great potential, and look at what she had done to herself. She'd had about as much volition as a cat in heat yowling in a Dumpster for something she did not understand. A runaway cat that had refused its tamed half-life for wilderness and want.

A tamed half-life was for idiots was what Andrei believed. That idea still makes Irina smile. She has to let go of this idea that Andrei's depravity somehow made him more genuine than other men. But she didn't know how to let go of that idea. She didn't know how to let go of any of Andrei's ideas. Or his voice. Or his eyes. Or the scent of him. Or the freedom she thought he gave her, the freedom to gleefully sink into the darkness and not care about any debts. The freedom to live in the red and be comfortable there.

Doi

Once upon a time something happened. Had it not happened, it would not be told. There was once an emperor who had so much money that he did not know what to do with it. Still, he was unhappy, for he had no children. No one could lift his mood, not even his formerly spirited wife.

Why are you so glum? he asked her one day.

My dear husband, I would like to take the carriage and go out for a ride.

Wait, I'll do better. I will build a ship for you.

He ordered a beautiful ship to be built, the most beautiful ever beheld. It was easier to look into the sun without being blinded than to look at this ship. Once it was finished, the emperor told his wife she could leave, as the ship was ready. Then he said: If you don't come back pregnant, do not come back.

So the empress journeyed on the ship with her favorite lady-in-waiting for many days, sweeping silently through the fog without sighting land. Then one day, the sun burned off enough of the mist that the empress could see an enormous palace emerging from the oblivion of the sea. She decided she must visit this marvel and replenish her ship's waning supplies. She sent her servant to the gates of the palace to query who lived there. When the sentry answered that this was the dwelling of the Mother of God, the servant did not dare go in. The empress pushed her aside and went through the gates herself.

In the courtyard was a tall, slender apple tree burdened with golden fruit. The empress was seized with a sudden need to eat one. She said to her servant, If I don't have one of those apples, I will die.

The servant was reluctant, but seeing her mistress growing ashen and ill, she went in and stole an apple as quickly as she could. When the empress ate the apple, she was suddenly dizzy with happiness, laying her hand on her swollen belly as the knowledge washed over her that she was six months pregnant. Let's go home at once, she said to her lady-in-waiting, for now my desire has been fulfilled.

But the Mother of God noticed that the most beautiful apple on her tree was missing. Who has stolen it? she asked the impassive sky. Then she spoke a curse: If a girl is born from this apple, she will be as beautiful as the sun—it would be easier to look into the sun without being blinded than to gaze at her face. But in her seventeenth year, she shall become a cat. She and everyone in her palace, thus cursed until an emperor's son comes and cuts off her head. Only then will they all become human again.

When the empress arrived home pregnant, there was much rejoicing. When the time came, she gave birth to a perfect little girl who was much loved by all who knew her. But on the day she became seventeen years old, she suddenly turned into a small, fire-eyed cat, sitting primly in the lush wreck of her shed princess robes. Throughout the palace, all the clothes of her subjects collapsed softly to the ground, from them emerging many lissome cats of all different colors and stripes.

Now in a faraway country there was an emperor with three sons. He had begun to drink when his wife died. Since he wanted to get rid of the burden of his children, he called them to him and gave them these orders: Every one of you shall go on a quest and bring me back a tribute so that I may see who is the biggest hero. Whoever is capable of bringing me linen so thin that it can be blown through the eye of a needle shall inherit my throne.

After a great farewell feast, the three princes separated, promising to meet again in a year. Each chose the way he wanted to go. The eldest chose a way where he would suffer hunger but his horse would have food. The only thing he met to take back to his father was a handsome little dog. The second brother chose a way where he had something to eat but his horse had nothing. He found a little shred of coarse linen that one could yank through the wide eye of a very big needle with a great deal of force and determination. One truly had to pull very hard.

The youngest brother traveled through a dark forest, his way difficult because of a heavy, hissing downpour that made it impossible for him to see his way ahead. For three days and three nights, the unrelenting rain came in sheets, making him grow desperate. On the morning of the third day, in a flash of lightning he saw a great palace straight ahead. He resolved to go to it, as he saw no other destination. But the door was closed, and all around was a high wall reaching up to heaven.

I am dying from hunger, the prince uttered in his loneliness, but nobody heard him. Suddenly, he saw dangling over the door a gleaming piece of meat that looked mighty juicy. In his yearning to feel something solid in his mouth, he leapt for it and the meat stuck to his hand, pulling him up and raising him high. When the prince tried to free himself, he found that the meat was a hard substance, its gleam that of precious stones rather than juices. He yelped in distress; a bell rang and he was unceremoniously dropped. As he dusted himself off, the door was opened slowly by an unseen hand. Our hero shrugged and said, Might as well.

Looking around the dim hallways, he saw not a single human being but eventually came upon a room with a candle and a bed. He decided to rest, as he was so weary, but no sooner had he touched the bed than ten disembodied hands appeared and began to beat him and tear away at his clothes. In his despair, the prince said, Oh Mother of God, who is beating me like this?

The hands stopped, leaving him completely naked. In a flash, food appeared at a table along with rich, finely wrought clothes. He dressed himself and feasted, and woke up the next morning refreshed. He decided to go on to the next room, and again the hands beat him and stripped him and the prince was fed and then clothed again, just as before. On the third day, he woke up surrounded by a dozen gray male cats, who guided him to a great hall where everything was made of pure gold. He was given an outfit of pure gold to wear to match the throne of pure gold where he was directed to sit, while a hundred cats sang and played music.

Our hero was wondering who ruled such a strange realm when he discovered a beautiful little cat with fire-colored eyes, her fur white as snow, lying in a golden basket. The cat empress pleased him greatly and he her, so she got up from her basket and declared to her subjects that the young man was her new consort. All the cats greeted him as their master. The empress of the cats rubbed her back sweetly against his hand and lay languorously across his lap, and then asked him, looking up at him with her blazing gaze, My dear hero, why have you come here?

My dear cat, God leads people down different paths, and my father has sent me to find linen so thin that it can be blown through the eye of a needle, and I have come to find that.

Meanwhile, the prince's two elder brothers had gone home and delivered their gifts while our hero sojourned at the cat palace. The father was much pleased by the handsome little dog, less so by the scrap of coarse linen. When he asked his sons where their younger brother was, they had to tell him that they did not know. It was assumed that he was dead and there was a great deal of mourning in the empire.

After many days, the cat said to the prince, My dear, don't you want to go home? The year of your quest is over.

No, I don't wish to go home. I am happy here. I'll stay here until my end.

No, you may not, replied the cat. If you want to stay here, you must first go back to your home and deliver your father what you promised.

But how can I find such thin linen with such fine threads?

Oh, that can be done.

It is not possible, my dear cat, that an entire year has gone by since I've been here.

Yes, even more. Time is different here. Since you left where you came from, nine years have passed.

How can one year be nine years? And then how many more years will it take me to go back?

Give me that whip hanging on the wall, the cat said. She cracked the whip in three directions, summoning a lightning carriage. They got into the carriage, and the cat asked the prince, Now are you ready to go home?

Before he could nod, the cat cracked the whip once more. A great white flash blotted everything out for an instant, and as the rolling thunder receded, the prince saw that he had now arrived at home.

Take this nut with you, the cat said, but don't open it until your father asks you to give him the linen.

When the prince entered the palace, he found everyone quite terrified at the great crash of his carriage's arrival. Yet his father did not waste any time, immediately asking his son whether he had brought something, whether he had found the linen. The prince said, Yes, father. With these words, he broke the nut by striking it with his sword. In the nut he found a kernel of maize. He broke that open and found a kernel of wheat. Then he got angry and complained, The damn cat has cheated me! The devil with the cat!

No sooner had he uttered these words that invisible claws were dragged across his hands, streaking them in blood. He dashed the kernel of wheat with the heel of his boot, and found inside it the tiny seed of a bothersome weed that crawls over walking paths. He hit that seed as well, and out of it exploded one hundred yards of the finest, whitest linen anyone had ever seen. The prince's father, stunned and delighted, declared that he must take the crown, having found the most beautiful linen.

No, father, the prince replied, I am rich enough. I already have an empire where I live and will go back there.

You cannot go back there yet, the father said, for each of you, my three sons, must now quest forth to find a wife.

All right, said the brothers, and they went.

The youngest brother got into the lightning carriage where the cat waited, and they went back to her realm. When they arrived, the cat asked what he had done, and he told her everything that had happened, and then said that he did not know how to find a wife. The cat listened carefully but said not a word. They lived together for another month, until one day she asked him, Don't you want to go home?

Oh, I don't want to go home, answered the prince. I have no reason.

In time, the two of them began to be in love with each other, unable to bear any time apart. One day, our young hero asked the cat, Why are you a cat?

Don't ask me yet, she replied. Ask me some other time. I hate to live in the world. Let's go together to your father.

Again she summoned the lightning carriage and took the prince home. When his father saw them, he said, Have you no wife? Why are you not married? Where is your wife?

His son showed him the cat and said, Here she is. This cat here.

The cat sat in her golden basket.

What do you want with a cat? the father shouted. You can't even talk with her.

At this the cat became angry. She jumped out of the basket and then did a somersault, which changed her into a dazzlingly beautiful girl with fiery hair. Our young hero laughed and embraced her. His brothers were completely petrified, but his father was so delighted with the beauty of his consort that he said, Truly, you have the most beautiful wife. You must become my successor and have my entire empire.

No, father, that won't do. I already have an empire and a crown, so give yours to my eldest brother.

While he spoke, the girl did a somersault, became a cat again, and lay in her golden basket.

When our hero and his consort were back in their palace, he was angry with her for still being a cat. She said, My dear, I will explain to you later why I have to be a cat. There's a curse on me.

For a while they lived in their cat empire as before, until one day the cat sharpened three yataghans. When the prince came home from hunting, she made a great show of pretending to be sick, rolling around and yowling pitifully. The prince tried to calm her, petting her and asking, My dear, what's the matter with you?

I'm very sick, she cried. If you love me and want to do something good for me, then cut off my tail. It's too big and heavy. I can't carry it anymore.

No, I can't cut you! You mustn't die; I would rather die myself. Here, I have a cream. I will heal you with that.

Yet she still insisted that he cut off her tail, and she broke his will. He finally did it, closing his eyes when the blade severed her flesh. When he opened his eyes, he gasped, for the cat had transformed into a girl up to the hips, while remaining a cat in her upper half. He was delighted with this development, but the cat didn't stop. She continued: I hate life. I don't want to go on living. Please cut my head off, and take over my whole empire.

How can you ask me to cut your head off?

If you love me and want to do something good for me, then cut my head off.

Finally he couldn't resist, so he gripped one of the yataghans tight and swiftly decapitated her. In that moment, she became totally a stunningly beautiful girl, and all the cats who were in the palace became human beings and the whole empire was redeemed as she was and everybody was delighted, though they would have to learn all over again how to make and wear clothes.

The cat empress who was now a girl kissed the prince in great happiness and said, From now on you are my husband. I was cursed by the Mother of God until an emperor's son would cut off my head. Now let's go to your father, but beware, he is dangerous.

When they went back to the prince's father, the old emperor fell in love with his son's fire-haired wife. When our hero was off hunting, the old man went to the beautiful wife's chamber, but there was a cat in his path on the way there. When he tried to take his daughter-in-law in his arms and tell her she should love him, she struck him across the cheek and hissed, What do you want, you old horror?

When the husband returned from his hunt, she told him what his father had done. He decided to leave at once, to go home—but his father came to him and said, If you don't let me have your wife, I'll hang you.

You know my wife will never let me die, the son said.

The father ordered his guard to seize the young couple and throw them in a dungeon, but they made their escape in the lightning carriage, the son's parting words to his father being: You know, father, it will not be long before my wife shall punish you.

When they got back to their empire, they mustered an enormous army and declared war on the father. What could the old emperor do? He had to march with his own army to do battle with the emperor of the cats. In three days, the army of the son had completely destroyed the army of the father. Only the father remained alive amid the butchered remnants of his forces. When he saw that he was lost and had no more strength, he said to his son: Please pardon me. It is true that I have made a bad thing happen, for had it not happened, it would not be told. Judge rightly, and rule my empire well.

Something was strange right away. It was more than the strangeness innate in being haunted by the tiny ghost of a person who never was. It was in the air. Andrei had come back from a meeting with Vasilii and had locked himself in his seldom-used office. Had Irina ever even seen that door locked? Dare she knock on it?

Yes.

"What is it?" Andrei's voice inside sounded remote.

"Andrei, what's going on?"

In response, the door swung open with deliberate slowness. Irina's first thought when she saw Andrei was that he was somehow not as tall as she had always thought he was. The look on his face was frank fear, fear without shield, without irony. Irina had difficulty believing her eyes.

"You have to leave," he said, as if he were a superstitious peasant and she the Gypsy who had knocked on his door in the dead of night.

"I'm sorry. If you're busy, we'll talk later."

"No, you don't understand. You have to *leave*."

He pushed so hard on the word *leave* that Irina started to understand what he meant. He meant be apart from him. Something contracted in the center of her, making a pain well up in the hollow of her chest.

"Leave for how long?"

"Leave for always."

The pain bloomed its way up to Irina's throat, leaving her unable to speak. Andrei sidled out of his office and shut the door behind him. He ushered her to the couch in the living room with the respectful gentleness of a funeral director. He put his hands on her shoulders, pushing her to sit her down. For a moment, she stood there looking furiously into his face. Then she relented. She sat down, and once she was settled he plopped down heavily next to her.

"It's for your own good. I'm sorry," he said.

"This is not how I thought we would part, Andrei."

"For your own safety, really, darling. You have to leave because I love you."

This was serious. This was deadly serious. He seldom resorted to telling her that he loved her.

"Why do I have to go? What is going on?"

Andrei shook his head slowly, his eyes looking anywhere but at her. The gray in his irises looked less like galvanized steel and more like dirty dish water. "I cannot tell you that."

"I can't just disappear. I have to say good-bye to Elena."

"No. She is gone."

Irina felt herself surrounded by a vast darkness, a lightlessness so deep that she could not distinguish a single shape or movement no matter how wide she tried to open her eyes. A lightlessness into which she reached out to feel only the movement of cold air. Her hand found nothing; there was no telling how big the darkness was.

"Andrei, is she dead?"

"She is gone."

The pain from Irina's heart spread through her limbs, knotting the muscles in her back and neck, throbbing into her brain. Irrepressible tears began to flow. She wished she could be a man right then, react to the world with the sneering distance it deserved.

"Irina, you still have the passport and card for Vasilica Andreescu. You have to give those back. If you left with them, it would be—it would be very bad."

"Andrei," she said through her tears, with audible anger.

He looked stricken. It was terrible to see him so helpless. Quite possibly his helplessness made her even angrier than the curt way she was being disposed of.

"Andrei, is this really how it ends?"

"I'm sorry."

She could not recollect ever hearing him apologize in earnest for anything, and now he had said he was sorry twice in the past five minutes. His apologies should have infected her with his fear. Right now, she should be afraid for her life. She sought the fear inside herself but it was nowhere to be found. What could she be afraid of now that she had loved the wrongest man on earth? What could they do to her that she hadn't done to herself?

"I am going to go," he said. "I cannot bear to watch you pack your things. When you are done, call Dragos. He will drive you to the airport. Get a ticket wherever you like. Do not tell him where you are going."

She opened her mouth to say something but he raised his hand to stop her from speaking. "And please, please," he said, "please do not tell me where you are going."

"If this is really how it ends," Irina said in a ragged voice as she began to cry in earnest, "then you must hold me one last time."

Andrei didn't answer, only arranged himself on the couch to let Irina settle into his arms. She sat on his lap like an outsize child as he snaked his hands around her waist. She leaned into his neck, her tears moistening the collar of his shirt. He gathered her tightly against his warm body.

The scent of him. How would she live without the scent of him?

"Andrei," she whispered.

"Darling?"

"Tell me a Romanian story."

"Once upon a time something happened. Had it not happened, it would not be told," he recited, and then fell silent.

Irina did not move, the hot tears flowing freely down her cheeks.

"A boy was born in a shithole village in a shithole country," he continued. "This boy was the bastard son of the village slut, with the dark skin of the Gypsy father who never acknowledged him. For a reason that could not be known, the woman who had the boy did not give him to the orphanage as she should have. She kept him and loved him the best she could but she was rough and simple. The other children, though they were born under an enlightened Communist leader who would march his country into a bright tomorrow, were still the little shit peasants they always were and hated the dark-skinned boy for his Gypsy looks. They hurled stones at him in the school recreation yard and called him a thief though the boy could not remember stealing anything. The boy was unhappy, but it didn't matter, because so was everybody else.

"On the weekends, when the boy was free from school, he was volunteered to sort the potato harvest for the government. For hours he did this, one stupid ugly dirty lump after another: which ones could be eaten, and which ones could not? He had to look for rot and disease. He made a pile of the good potatoes and a pile of the sick ones. The government, in its magnanimous kindness, in its infinite munificence, allowed the boy to take home the spoiled potatoes as a reward for his earnest labor. His mother would mash them up and try to make something edible out of them, because they were hungry. They were hungry, but of course it did not matter, because so was everybody else.

"One day, as he sifted through the potatoes, the boy said to himself, Fuck this. Fuck this shit life. Fuck these little assholes saying that I steal. If they are going to think that I steal, then I might as well. I might as well proudly wear the names they call me.

"This moment of wisdom granted the boy the courage to put the best potatoes in his knapsack to take home to his mother. His mother said nothing about the superior quality of his haul, at the crisp unmarred flesh of the stolen potatoes. She did not say thank you for the good eating; she did not chide him for doing something he should not have. So, he continued to do this because the mash his mother made was tasty that week. He continued to do this and nobody bothered to catch him. He learned that it was easy to make yourself less hungry as long as you dared.

"Over the years, the boy became a lad. It was time for him to leave school and get work at a factory. His last day going through potatoes, the boy said to himself: A factory? Fuck this shit life. Fuck making myself less hungry. I want to feast.

"This moment of wisdom granted the boy the courage to steal a nice sack of bribery money from the mayor to go to America. There the lad would become a man and learn how to feast. It is not known whether he lived happily ever after, but at least he wore nice clothes and drove a nice car and wiped his ass with nice toilet paper. He even bought factories in his shithole country just to show the peasants he could own them, though he never bothered to go back again to say so to their faces. He ate and fucked his fill until he died, and that must have been a kind of happiness, no?"

Irina looked at Andrei's face when she heard the rising inflection of his question. She had stopped crying while listening to him. He looked back into her big, beautiful young eyes and smiled. He cupped her cheek with his hand.

"I might have made a mistake, darling," he said. "I am not sure that was the Romanian story you asked for. I might have just told you an American story."

She gave him a kiss that said, Make love to me one last time. It was the desperate kiss of a prisoner about to be executed. But he did not open his mouth against the pressure of her lips. That aborted kiss, Andrei's refusal, was the worst thing that has happened to Irina. Her tears returned, springing stingingly from her blurring eyes, now that she knew her body would never open for him again. Her body was abandoned by the only thing it had ever loved. She felt herself hollowing out, felt herself become certain that she would be empty forever.

Of course, all the pain is her fault. Her fault for being unhinged enough to kiss him in the first place.

All this time, these two years spent with Andrei, and all it came down to in the end was two suitcases. The only things she owned were clothes, and she'd decided not to take most of those. They were all from Andrei anyway, so did she really own them? She took none of the lingerie, none of the pretty things she used to wear to turn his head. She was quite sure she wouldn't be able to stomach looking at lingerie again, much less wear it.

Dragos was on his way to fetch her, in the sports car a stupid boy had tried to steal. Was that boy's body decomposing somewhere?

If she wanted to do one last thing in this apartment where she had lived with Andrei, now was the time.

The office was unlocked.

The first place Irina looked was the desk drawer where she'd found the gun. The green folders were still there, but the gun was gone. In its place she lay the passport with her picture in it that bore some other girl's name. Tucked into the passport was the bank card. She'd thought of taking Vasilica with her, but the time for Vasilica was over. The nonexistent girl was not the thing to take with her. She wanted to take something that would *perhaps* result in death, not *certainly*. What she really wanted to take was something that would make Andrei come and get her. She shut the drawer on Vasilica Andreescu.

She had carved the life out of the center of her so that she could stay, and now they were making her go anyway.

When she'd asked Andrei what was the strangest thing about

America when he got here, he'd said the choice. Everything that was wrong with America he could get used to. But the choice, the dizzying, nearly limitless choice—it was the choice that drew him, that scared him most.

Irina opened the small metal cabinet. She looked over the numbers on the tags attached to each key. Her favorite was 21012 because it read the same backward and forward. Like the end of a countdown that decided to turn around at zero and count back up again. This was the one.

She could have made the choice to leave that key alone. She could have made the choice to have the baby, if she'd really wanted to. Why did these choices not feel like choices then? Why did it feel as though all the wrong things she had ever done were inevitabilities written in her very blood?

Irina pocketed the little golden key. She did not, at that moment, particularly intend to go find what the key unlocked and look inside.

She opened the desk drawer back up and pulled the green folder that bore the same number as the key. Inside the folder there was the address of a bank in a city far away.

Andrei had told her not to tell anyone where she was going. Well, she wasn't going to say a word. She was just going to take a key and the name of an American city with her. She would leave the folder behind to make sure Andrei knew which key was missing.

If he wanted it back, then he would have to come find her.

Dragos drove Irina to the airport in silence. She wanted to ask him a thousand questions, but the stormy look on his face dissuaded her. She thought he might leave her at the curb without a word, but instead of pulling up to the airport's drop-off area, he pulled into a spot in short-term parking.

"Are you coming in with me?" Irina asked tentatively.

"No, I do not want a public good-bye. But I did want a minute."

Irina looked around. It was dim, and there were nothing but empty cars around. As isolated places went, this was a fairly decent one for a quick execution. It was unlikely that anyone would hear a gunshot. But then there was the problem of disposing of the body. He'd have to drive back out of the airport with her in the car. Or he'd have to dump her lifeless mass right there in the parking lot. No, this was logistically not very clever. Besides, Dragos would never subject his car to all the gore.

Still, when he reached inside his jacket to pull something out, Irina's heart skipped a beat.

But it was not a gun. It was a small, neat packet of hundred-dollar bills.

"This is for you," he said, "to get you started where you are going."

She did not yet have the banker's eye that would have gauged the packet was worth about ten thousand dollars. She did not yet have the banker's hand that would gladden that the bills were old bills, which would make them easier to count.

"I've never seen so much cash at once," Irina said stupidly.

Dragos did not answer, only reached for Irina's purse and tucked the money into it. She would count it later in a bathroom stall while waiting for her plane and realize the amount was the same as what Dragos had offered Andrei to take her to bed. Was the money a gift from Andrei or from Dragos? Maybe it was better not to know.

She did not say thank you, only looked into Dragos's face. He smiled a disconcerting smile. It looked almost sheepish. Before she could respond, he reached across the car and held her tightly. She allowed him to. She even put her arms around him. She pulled away from his embrace when she felt something hard on his back.

"It's a gun," he explained when she looked at him questioningly. "I carry it all the time now."

This must have been why the gun was missing from Andrei's desk drawer. It must have been that he was carrying it all the time now too.

"Are you in danger?" Irina asked.

"Irina, it is best for you not to tangle with the likes of us anymore. Go out there and be good. Go back to university."

This might have been the strangest moment of this whole strange trip, Dragos giving Irina sound life advice. He laughed at the look she was giving him. Before she could say anything, he got out and pulled her suitcases out of the small, crowded trunk of his speedy roadster. She stepped out of the car slowly, as if moving under water. He was about to open the door to get back in and leave her there alone in the parking lot when she put her hand on his arm.

"Elena," she said.

"Andrei didn't tell you?"

Irina shook her head.

"Maybe he thought it would make you safer not to know. But she was your friend, so you should know. She left. She stole a truly ludicrous amount of money from Vasilii and left. Vasilii thinks that because you were friends you know where she went. He was going to put you to the question."

Irina opened her mouth as if to say something, but nothing came out. Elena wasn't dead. Elena had put one over on the butcher scribe himself. The world had taken a funny turn.

Before Dragos drove away, he gave Irina a wet smooch on the cheek and whispered in her ear, "My little philosopher."

In the air, everything felt different. The constant roar of the jet engine, the hot cottony feel of the recycled air, the drowsy proximity of so many bodies, the fluorescent half-light—all these things tamped down the intensity of Irina's feelings. It was like being in a sort of stasis. Perhaps being so far from the ground put her above her troubles. Even the knowledge that she would eventually have to land seemed remote.

The in-flight movie was on. Sometimes she looked at the mute people agitating themselves onscreen and dimly wondered what their fuss was about, but mostly she stared at nothing. Elena is alive, she kept telling herself. Elena is alive, maybe flying through the sky somewhere right now. Elena is rich.

Irina had been ejected from her wayward life by a cataclysm and Elena was right at the center of it. Elena had saved her. She would only think of this years later, when she would be able to think of her departure as being saved.

Andrei had saved her by sending her away. It might have been his one act of true love.

When Irina had told Elena to leave, Elena had said *not yet*. Only later, up in the air, did Irina finally hear this *not yet*. Elena had let Vasilii cut her up because she was biding her time all along in order to execute the most magnificent, wily heist imaginable. She might have been waiting until her family was somewhere safe before striking. Vasilii's wife had put her dainty finger on the lighter side of the world's rigged scale, making it only slightly awry in the smallest possible way. The scale was not tipped visibly. But Irina had felt the weight shift. She hoped that Vasilii had given Elena a false passport with a false name too, and that the false identity he had forced on her had been the tool she used to pluck him like a chicken. Elena had not done what she'd been told. She had been bold, and now she was gone. Not cast out like Irina, but a triumphant gone. Not a victim of the butcher scribe but his undoing.

The flight attendant asked if Irina wanted a drink. Irina looked up at her dumbly for a moment and then asked for a glass of wine. The attendant did not move, looking into Irina's face with visible suspicion.

"I'm going to have to see some identification," she said pleasantly.

Out here in the big world, a girl of Irina's youth needed a valid piece of identification displaying a legal age in order to get a drink. She had forgotten. She had forgotten the great big world.

"I'll just have a Coke," Irina said with a sigh.

The attendant plunked the soda in front of her with indifference and moved on. This was what young people drank out here in the big, visible world. The can was coated with a cold dew. It cracked and hissed when she opened it. The bubbly sweetness tickled her tongue. Vasilii would not track Elena, find her, and chop her into pieces left to desiccate in some hole in the desert. Elena would forever be sipping a gaudily colored drink with a paper parasol in it, on some faraway tropical beach. This is the story Irina would keep telling herself.

She took the little golden key out of her pocket. It was an utterly stupid and dangerous thing she had done, but somehow it felt less dangerous than being ejected into the big world by herself with nothing to run to. How far could she be flung if there was no past for ballast? She wasn't like Elena. She hadn't come to steal. She'd come to give herself and they'd turned her away.

After Irina drank down the last dregs of the soda, she did something she did not expect to do. She closed her eyes and fell asleep. In her dream, a man made love to a girl. The light was warm; the colors were saturated. It was as if the dream was on film, had been art-directed. The costuming for the girl was careful and exquisite: the man slowly divested her of the most beautiful designer lingerie money could buy. The first thing he took off was her high heels, with the care of Prince Charming fitting a delicate shoe to Cinderella's dainty foot in reverse. It was clear that the man loved the girl very much. It was also clear that he owned her.

It feels good to dissolve. It feels good to put oneself in the hands of another and forget everything. It feels good to be nothing but feeling, to have no boundaries, to be no one. At that moment the girl could be any girl. She could be all girls at once. It did not matter whose face she wore. It did not matter if her face was Irina's face, or Elena's face, or the face of some nameless orphan with a broken life any more than it mattered whether the man's face was Andrei's face, or Vasilii's face, or the face of some nameless father who would never acknowledge any child he mistakenly conceived. None of the things that mattered in the big, visible world mattered here, in this utterly naked place.

She would always remember. Inside Irina, the man would make love to the girl forever. The best Irina could do to attempt to go on with her life was to try not to watch.

Unu

The image now in question is the portrait of a man made legend. For centuries, historians have looked upon this portrait and speculated on the cruelty in the man's narrow blade face, the distant determination in his shifting eyes, the depraved sensuality in the curve of his lip. Lean closer and ask yourself what the image says. If you put your heated cheek close enough to its cool surface to see the streaks of every brushstroke with your inquiring eye, maybe the image will be kind enough to talk to you. Maybe the image, in its infinite wisdom, will say: Once upon a time something happened. Had it not happened, it would not be told.

Over a besieged land surrounded by three hostile kingdoms reigned a voivode called the Dragon. One day the Dragon gave his allegiance to one of the three kingdoms, the next day to another, the next day to another—all to keep his land from being swallowed by whichever of the three kingdoms was the hungriest. Eventually his dealings caught up with him, and he was betrayed by his boyars to the sultan of the greatest of the three hostile kingdoms. He and his eldest son were put to death, his other son put in prison. His second son moldered in jail, reigning over only his cell, executing the insects who crawled in the straw he slept on by crushing them with his heels and dispensing punishment to the mice who gnawed on his crust of bread by running his dull knife through their small bodies. He passed much time watching them wiggle on his blade, watching the life dim from their beady black eyes.

Eventually his star rose again and he took his father's land under the name Son of the Dragon. He gave his allegiance to none of the three hostile kingdoms. When ambassadors were sent to collect tributes, he refused to pay. When the ambassadors would not take off their hats to salute him, he had the hats nailed to their heads and sent them away. He raised a great army and won many battles. He became known far and wide for how much pain he could inflict on the bodies of those who would not yield to his rule. Thieves seldom dared practice their trade within his domain. In the central square of his capital city, Son of the Dragon displayed a golden cup on an open altar. Such was the fear he inspired that none dared steal or even touch the cup. It was said that whoever drank from the cup would kiss the lips of Justice.

One day Son of the Dragon wished to examine the precise manner of his elder brother's death, having not seen it with his own eyes. He ordered the corpse exhumed from the unmarked grave in the public burial ground. Upon opening the coffin he found his brother lying facedown, his body contorted and his mouth open as if gasping for breath. Deep grooves from the dead prince's fingernails were gouged in the coffin's lid. The voivode said nothing. He closed the lid and called a great celebration for Easter Sunday, inviting all the boyars of the land to his feast.

On Easter morning the boyars came to the royal garden, mounted on fine horses and riding in carriages. Their wives brought fine oriental carpets to rest and converse on. Everyone wore their brightest, most beautiful clothes. The palace provided roasted lambs, sweet cakes, and mulled wines for the feast and Gypsy fiddlers for the music. The voivode did not eat and did not dance, watching silently over the revelry. As the sun sank behind the mountains and the people reeled in their most frenzied joy and forgetfulness, Son of the Dragon signaled the captains of the guard, who sealed the doors to the royal garden. At his command, they seized all the boyars who were old enough to remember the killing of the Dragon and his eldest son. As all the women and young ones were made to watch, stakes were driven through the bodies of the old betrayers, from the fundament up through the mouth, the neck, or the shoulder. The stakes were cut with dull points so as not to pierce the vital organs but move them aside, so that death would not come quickly.

The stakes were raised, and as the writhing bodies of the boyars slowly slid down the shafts, the night was filled with their howls and groans. The voivode looked upon his work and said, Listen to them—what music they make! Send the fiddlers home, for this is all I need.

With these words, he sat down to feast, and ordered the boyars' wives and young ones to eat with him. Stupefied with terror, they did as he said, looking down at the victuals they could not get themselves to swallow. One young man closed his eyes so that he would not have to look at the agonies of his father, putting his hand over his nose and mouth to stop the terrible stench of clotting blood and emptied bowels. The voivode saw and told the two guards at his side, Skewer him on a stake taller than all the others, so that the disagreeableness will not reach his delicate nostrils. And bid my steward to go to the central square and bring me my golden cup.

As his orders were followed, soldiers rounded up everyone they had not impaled by the garden gates and manacled them together. Once they were all in chains, the voivode took the golden cup that the steward had handed him and stood at the feet of the dying lad on the tallest stake. He held up the chalice and in it gathered some of the thick, pouring blood. He raised it to the company and wished them Godspeed on their journey, and then explained to them that they would walk fifty miles to the mountain, where they would build him a castle. They would work until all their Easter finery had rotted off their bodies. And then they would work some more, until the castle was finished. All those who were left alive then could go home to their estates. Was he not clement?

He stood holding his cup, listening to the groans of the boyars up on their stakes harmonize with the clamor of the weeping women and young ones as they were being pushed by the soldiers out of the garden and onward to their toils. Once the gates were shut after them, he turned to the forest of dying bodies, looked into the eyes of the father crying out for death as he twisted on his stake, drank the son's blood from the chalice, and fainted.

In his dream, Son of the Dragon was kissed awake by the warm, plush lips of a beautiful woman. She had eyes as clear as a mountain stream and a gleaming abundance of fiery hair.

Then it is true what they say, whispered the voivode. You must be Justice.

That is one of my names, answered the beautiful woman. I am here to give myself to you.

The voivode, heartened by her words, put his hand on her to unlace her girdle. She slapped his grasp away as if he were a brazen child, and said merrily, That is not the way Justice gives herself—not to you, anyway.

The voivode wanted to crush her white throat with his smarting hand for her insolence, but found that he could not move. A glowing heat, not entirely unpleasant, bewitched him into stillness. Justice laughed melodiously. Voivode, she said, there are so many wonders in store for you in the next life. When you shed the shell of your body you will not drift into merciful sleep like all those you have staked. You will remain awake to haunt the nightmares of peasant children. You will remain awake to witness your name rolling down through the centuries.

As it should be, said the voivode.

As it should be, answered Justice, the touch of her hand making the heat grow inside the man's body until it hovered at the edge of pain, making his back arch slightly. As it should be, you will remain alive in the stories they will tell about you. As it should be, illustrious conqueror, the people of the world will dream you sleepless forever. From one mind to the next you will grow new limbs and have old limbs cut; your shape will never be at rest. One day in a country far away, a storyteller will slip his kingdom's pent-up sex into your ecstatic violence and your name will roar across the world, voivode; you will take whatever shape they give you, voivode; you will be forced to incarnate the stickiest of forbidden longings, the dankest of all fears. You will be an image to make matrons shrivel in horror in the dryness of their old age, to make virgin girls swoon for the embrace of inoffensive lovers never bold enough to penetrate them, to make the diseased squirm in pleasure at the thought of all that blood—all that blood, voivode. You will dissolve in all their blood and all their blood will thrum through you, as it should be, great and mighty warrior, as it should be. You will never be granted peace, you will never sleep—

As Justice spoke these words, the heat in the man's body gathered at his center, a great blazing shaft of agony burning inside him from his loins to his mouth. He wanted to thrash and claw the earth but he was pinned where he lay, the only movement allowed him a rising tremor as the future ripped its way through all his flesh—the future, the future, the great inexorable restless terrifying future. He tried to open his mouth to scream but could not. Instead Justice held him tightly and planted a hard kiss on his frozen lips, sending a blast of lightning so powerful into him that everything went black.

Never sleep again, her voice said, in the sighing tones of a woman well pleased.

Son of the Dragon awakened with a great start, his body covered with blood and mire. The huge smothering gray sky teased his hot tingling skin with a few cool droplets. His body was in a state of tight, unbearable arousal. He sat up and looked around at the forest of torn, dying bodies, his mind swirling with confusion, his heart racing with unaccountable speed. There had been a dream. What dream? Whose dream?

Did it matter? The voivode stood up and strode toward the castle, his flesh humming with animal heat, calling for his servants, calling for his sword, calling for a woman, calling for everything in this life that pleased him best.

1

Irina has reached zero. All the rows of numbers she has typed in neatly add up to nothing. Her cash is balanced for the day, to the penny. She stares at the 0 in the lower right corner of the screen. It looks expectant and open, as if waiting to be fed. The other tellers have balanced and gone. The other officers left Amy in charge of shutting down the closed bank for the night.

"We're done, right?" Amy says wearily as they lock up Irina's cashbox inside the vault. "We fed the ATMs."

"We didn't do the night deposit."

"Fuck. The night deposit."

Amy looks so exhausted and demoralized that Irina has to ask what is the matter.

"It's…it's kind of personal," Amy says, sighing.

Irina waits quietly while Amy locks up the enormous mechanism of the heavy vault door. The huge bolt clanging shut inside sounds like finality.

"Not that something being inappropriate usually stops me

from saying it," Amy observes, and gives a weak titter. "Okay. I'll tell you. I'm the worst person in the world."

"That," Irina says with some authority, "I doubt very much."

Amy waves off Irina's assessment and starts her story without prompting. "Before I came to this city to work at this shitty bank, I lived with a man. He was a good one. I wasn't living with him for all that long before I got sick. Really sick, for a long time. I shat blood, I puked shit—every fucked-up thing a body could do to itself, my body went and did it. There was a lot of pain. There were lots of drugs. I had doctors put lots of things in various holes. I had other holes cut into me so that the doctors could put more stuff in them too. I lost fifty pounds. I fainted every time I stood up. There were lots of heavy drugs. I cried a lot, when I had the energy. I thought I was going to die. Did you know the human body can die of pain? Even if you're not actually dying per se, if you are in enough pain for enough time, say for years, you will fade away eventually. Your digestion slows. Your heart slows. Also the drugs help. For a long time, they didn't even know what was the matter with me. At first they said it was in my head, the fuckers. Two years of this shit."

"What was it? The disease."

"It doesn't matter, really. What matters is that this man I lived with stuck by me through all this nightmare. He drove me to the emergency room more times than I can remember. He held my hand and told me it was going to be all right even when we both knew that it wasn't. He watched my body, this body that was supposed to turn him on and make him happy, fall apart and waste away and become an object of degradation and pain. Lots of times, I counted my morphine pills to see if

I had enough to off myself, but then I thought of him coming home and finding my dead body and I couldn't do it. How did he stay through all that? He stayed with me through it all, Irina. He was there when I woke up from the last surgery, the one that finally helped. He was there with a little pot of pink miniature roses. He must have gotten them from the hospital store. They were scrawny, miserable-looking flowers and they didn't smell like anything, but they were alive. He took me home and helped me to the toilet and fetched me food and took care of me until I was better. If watching your body die is some crazy shit, watching your body un-die is even crazier. He was with me through all this shit. When this shit ended we could have gotten married and had a real life. But once I was better, do you know what I did?"

"What?" Irina whispers.

"I left."

The silence in the bank is hermetic. Outside there is a world, but it cannot get in.

"Can you believe I left him after that? How much do I suck? He saved my life every day for two years, probably so I could be his wife one day, and then I left him."

"But why?"

"I'm telling you, I'm the worst person in the world."

Irina wants to say that she has quite possibly met the worst person in the world, and he wasn't Amy. But maybe Amy needs to believe in her horribleness. That belief is the justice she dispenses to herself. She speaks fast, trying to explain.

"I couldn't. I just couldn't stay. He was so good to me that whole time and he was good to me after, but his face—all I saw in it was my time suffering and slowly decaying into an early grave. The pills and the pain and the slow coming apart. He had the sweetest eyes but my fucking death was in his eyes. That's what I saw when I looked at him, the slow process of dying. And here I was alive, and mostly all right, and here he was reminding me of all the dying."

"You left to start over," Irina says.

"I broke his heart."

There is another silence. Then Irina tries to tell Amy that what she did doesn't make her the worst person in the world, but Amy snaps, "You can't tell me what I did was right."

"You did what you had to, Amy."

"But what I had to do was so shitty!"

Amy bursts into tears like a heartbroken child. Irina stands there flummoxed for several seconds, and then goes to her and awkwardly encircles her with her arms. It's normal, right? Just two bankers working late and weeping on each other. Inappropriate confessions are, after all, a matter of course in the vault. Except they aren't in the vault. Well, no matter. They are *near* the vault.

"Amy," Irina says, rubbing her back in a way that she hopes translates as soothing. "Please don't worry so much. You're okay. You're not the worst person in the world."

"So, what am I, then?"

Irina gives this question careful consideration in the time required to take a deep breath and slowly let it out again. Then she delivers her verdict: "You're just a garden-variety asshole like the rest of us."

Amy laughs amid her tears. "Now that," she says, "that sounds like the kind of shit I might say."

"I know. That's why I said it."

Amy's crying dies down. She wipes at her eyes with the heels of her hands with quick sweeps as if embarrassment is beginning to descend on her. "All right," she says after letting out a deep sigh. "Let's do the night deposits."

"Look, just go home. I'll do them."

"But I'm the officer," Amy protests weakly. "I have the key for that box."

"Give me the key and I will leave it in your desk after I'm done."

This is how Irina comes to be left entirely alone in the bank, after Amy waves good-bye when ushered gently out. It's very rare for a banker to be alone in a bank. It's practically unheard of for a teller to be in such a situation. A lower. Only uppers have the keys to the front door; uppers are the ones who let the lowers in.

When the glass door clicks shut in the darkening evening separating the two bankers, both still think they will see each other the next morning.

The creaky hinge yawns open. Irina reaches into the metal box and pulls out a few packets. Fortunately, there is not a lot of cash to count in the night deposits. The merchants have left mostly checks today. She sits at Amy's desk to do her tabulating. When she drops Amy's key in the top drawer of the desk, it makes a sonorous *ting* against some loose change left scattered among the pencils and Post-its. Irina stares at the key amid the office jetsam. It is small and silver-colored. Perfectly nondescript. It looks like a lot of other keys that open a lot of other locks in this bank, like for instance the little key Irina taunts herself with. Why has she played with herself for so long? What has she been waiting for?

Amy died and then un-died and then left the life that was given back to her. She left because she had to.

Elena, too, left when it was time, because she had to.

Irina was the only one who hadn't left when she had to. She left her good life because she felt like it, because she didn't want to be a good girl. Then, when she had to leave the bad life, she found that she couldn't. Even now she still clings to it. She's kept that goddamn key, consigning herself to limbo by being too chicken to look into the box that the key is supposed to open.

That whole time, she has waited here with her little talisman key for the bad life to come back to her. She still misses Andrei so much. Andrei, who, with his refusal to come for her and take her back, or shoot her for her theft, has effectively given her the contents of his safe-deposit box. It is another gift she could turn away.

But before she turns it away, she might at the very least take a little look at it.

Irina puts the bank's key in the left lock of the safe-deposit box. She puts her little golden key in the right lock. She turns them both. Their action is smooth and noiseless, as are the well-oiled hinges of the little metal door when she swings it open.

Where is Andrei? Is he dead? Is Dragos? Did Vasilii, in his cold storm of anger, shoot them both?

Or worse, has Andrei completely forgotten her?

She pulls out the reinforced box. It is very heavy. At least it's not empty. Wouldn't emptiness be the world's finest joke?

She opens the lid.

She recognizes the smell of what is inside before her brain even tells her what her eyes are looking at.

No. Impossible.

And yet—of course.

The box is filled to the brim with tidily stacked packets of hundred-dollar bills. Just stupid, stupid cash like the stuff she counts every day for her stupid, stupid job. No drugs, no jewels, no deeds to ancestral lands. No fake identities nor real ones. Just Benjamin Franklin's placid, sideways gaze looking at her from countless little pieces of numbered paper, as if asking her, What did you expect? Did you expect to find something that meant something? Well, no luck. It's only me again. Money. Just a bunch of paper printed with my dead face.

They are brand-new bills, ordered by serial number in neat packets held together by straps of paper. Just like a fresh shipment from the Federal Reserve printing press. This means that if someone cared, someone could keep track of the numbers on the bills and trace them. There is no doubt in Irina's mind that nobody cares. No one will bother tracing her.

She can smell that the bills are genuine; she doesn't need to fetch the pen with the gold-hued ink that turns blackish blue when it is swept across a counterfeit bill. Goddamn—it's all new bills. They'll stick together; they'll cut her when she counts them. The smell of the bills' ink will be on her hands; only lemon juice will get that smell off. The cleansing will sting the hell out of the tiny, invisible cuts in the delicate skin of her palms.

Judging by the volume, Irina's banker's eye tells her there is a good million dollars in there in uncirculated money that has passed through no hands, that has not yet touched the world. Money that belongs to nobody.

No. No fucking way, Amy would say.

She has to laugh. She hopes they aren't dead. She hopes they are all thriving off their ill-gotten gains. She hopes Andrei still traffics whatever he has always trafficked, that he remains as eternally unchanged as a fairy tale. She hopes Elena is walking down a street somewhere wearing a string of large, blushing pearls, matching earrings, a lavender sapphire on her right hand, and a ruby on her left—like a woman betrothed on both sides. She hopes wherever Elena is, she has whatever she wants. She hopes that after seven years unfound, she will become human again. She hopes there will be children, and that these children will not be revenants.

Irina leaves one packet of the hundred-dollar bills in the top drawer of Amy's desk. Ten thousand dollars, the same amount Dragos had given her when they parted. She thinks of leaving it there without explanation. Then it occurs to her that this might be too confusing. Amy would be liable to turn over this unknown money to some authority somewhere, especially after it became clear that Irina would not come back. That wouldn't do when it is a gift.

Irina does the only thing she knows how to do to make money mean something.

She writes on it, one line on each of the first ten bills in Amy's packet, like pages from a children's storybook:

Amy, this is for you.
It is not the bank's, it's mine to give.
Now it's yours.
Don't tell anybody about it.
I am sorry that I couldn't give notice and

I am sorry
that I had to take the bags for the night deposit.
Amy
you are a fine person
Be good.

Zero

The Roman emperor Trajan commissioned this image to commemorate a victory. Carved in stone, clean-shaven soldiers on horseback surround a barbarian scrabbling on his knees. The soldiers brandish shields and lances. The barbarian, head turned to face his captors, slashes his own throat. Such was the fall of a rebel province at the edge of the Roman Empire. Dacia, the province was named.

Once upon a time something happened.

Nearly two thousand years later, the cornered barbarian king would be carved in stone again, forty meters tall on the bank of the Danube, by a nation that declared itself descended from Dacia. He would be stately this time, impassively watching the flow of the river from the side of the mountain. The nation that claims itself descended from Dacia speaks a language that is mostly Roman, leavened by the tongues of other conquerors. Of Dacian nothing is left, save possibly a few words that cannot be traced to any other language.

Had it not happened, it would not be told.

Decebalus is the name of the vanquished Dacian king who dared rise against the Romans. This is what history says. It carves itself in stone; it counts on the stone never crumbling.

On this contested land that now calls itself Romania, before it was washed over in blood by wave after wave of conquerors, before it was trodden by Dacians even, there lived a peaceful people with no name. Among this tribe, no one ever died. They did not know what dying meant. Only every now and then, a beautiful woman came and called one of them, and whoever followed her never returned.

One warm spring, a man from the outside came and settled with his family among the nameless people. He heard of the beautiful woman and could not wonder enough at the stupidity of those who followed her. He resolved that neither he nor anyone in his family would ever follow anyone who called them, no matter who it might be. He advised everyone who would listen never to follow anyone who called them if, as he said, they did not want to die. No one listened to the stranger's strange words and everything went on as before. That is, until one day seven winters hence, when, as the outside man and his family were sitting comfortably in their house, his wife suddenly began to shout, I'm coming! I'm coming! while putting on her fur coat. Her husband seized her by the hand and reproached her: What are you doing, madwoman? Stay here, if you don't want to die!

Don't you hear how she is calling me? I'll only see what she wants and come back at once, the wife said, struggling to escape from her husband's grasp. He held her fast as he managed to bolt all the doors in the room. Seeing herself trapped, the wife said, Let me alone, husband. I don't care about going now.

The man thought she'd come to her senses, so he loosened his grip on her. As soon as she felt his hand slacken, she wrenched herself from him and threw open the door, running outside. Her husband followed, pulling her back by her fur coat and entreating her not to go. The wife shrugged off the coat, leaving him standing there with his stunned hands gripping her shed garment, and disappeared into the cold night, her voice fading into the distance as she sang out to her seducer, I'm coming! I'm coming!

When she was gone and all was quiet, the husband collected himself, went back to the house, and told his children, If you're mad and want to die, go. In God's name, I can't help you. I've told you often enough that you must follow no one, no matter who calls you.

More days passed—many days, weeks, months, and years—and the peace in the outside man's household was not disturbed again.

Then one morning, when he visited his barber's as usual to be shaved, just as the barber was about to lay the blade on his throat, the outside man began to shout, I won't come, do you hear? I won't come!

The barber and his customers all stared. The man, looking piercingly at the open door as if someone was framed there, said, Take notice once and for all that I won't come, and go away from here.

He became increasingly restless, and then cried out, Go away, do you hear? Go away if you want to keep all your pretty skin, for I tell you a thousand times I won't come!

He continued to rave at the open door about being left in peace, finally springing up and snatching the razor from the barber's hand and leaping out the door, slashing at the air at the person calling him whom nobody else could see. The barber, who did not want to lose his razor, followed. The man ran and the barber pursued, until they were out of the village. Into the dark woods they went. There the man fell into a chasm from which he did not come out again, so that, like all the rest, he had followed the voice that called him.

The barber returned home, beside himself, and told everybody he met what had happened. So the belief spread through the land that the people who had gone away and not returned had fallen into that yawning gulf, for until then no one had known what had become of those who followed the voice of the beautiful woman.

The men from the village formed a search party to visit the scene of the misfortune, to see the insatiable chasm that swallowed up all the people and yet never had enough. Nothing was found. It looked as if, since the beginning of the world, nothing had been there except a broad, open plain. From that day forward, the peaceful people without a name lost their peace and began to die like all people from all time. Like we all must.

2

Irina will later reflect that, of course, there could have been nothing but money in that safe-deposit box. There was no way that the box was going to yield anything illuminating; that fantasy was all hers. It will take her several months of aimless traveling to reach this conclusion. It will come to her while lying fully dressed on a generic hotel coverlet, looking up at the blank white ceiling, the grainy chocolate the maid had left on her pillow slowly melting on her tongue. Not quite communist chocolate, but close.

Somewhere out in the great big world, Elena is in another anonymous room with hotel chocolate dissolving in her mouth—this is what Irina will tell herself. She will tell herself that her double is out there doing all the same things that she does, except with more purpose and panache. She will hold on to the idea that there is someone out there who is better at being her than she is. Someone who knows what to do with the money. The heavy, unwieldy cash she drags everywhere and spends apologetically, both boon and embarrassment.

When all that is left of the chocolate is the taste, Irina will sit up on her undisturbed bed and call her parents. A few days later, she will even visit them. They will not quite know what to do with her; maybe they will even be a bit afraid to touch her, as if she has returned not quite herself. They will ask her if she is all right, if she needs money. She will tell them she doesn't need any money, she has plenty. They will want to know where she went, what she's been doing, and why she doesn't need any money. She will give them the silence they know so well, the refusal she's had in her since she was a tiny child afraid of colors. They will suggest that she go back to the university to finish her degree. She will think about this suggestion and come to the conclusion that *going back* to anything is not what she wants at the moment. Going back doesn't seem as though it's any use.

She could take a plane to Romania. She could sleuth out which orphanage she came from. Would someone answer when she knocked on the door? Would someone recognize her sad blue eyes and take her to a gray little room and say, Look, this is where you used to sleep? What would this get her?

The place is probably an empty ruin anyway. She would walk into a dilapidated building looking for a past and no past would come to her. She would only frighten a homeless child huffing paint from a plastic bag in a dark corner. The story would refuse her an ending. She would not even crumble to dust. She would merely walk out again, stand in the hollow entryway looking out into a sunless, mild day. There would be illegible graffiti in a foreign language on the wall next to her. Even if she could read it, it would make no difference, would tell her nothing.

This would have been a good time to be a smoker; it would have been the moment to light a cigarette and squint in a mildly pained way as she inhaled. It would give her something to do with her hands.

She waited for them and they didn't come for her, she would think. A small cat would come around the street corner to soundlessly sit at the foot of a tree. It would look at her with its fiery orange eyes. It would not be an enchanted fairy-tale princess; its fur would not be a luminous white. A mottled, greasy-looking calico, gangly-limbed and not yet full-grown, but no longer a kitten. Soon the cat, a she—Irina knows all calico cats are female—would start to yowl in the night until some passing tom made her heavy with young.

The cat would lick her forepaw and pass it several times over her head, to reach behind her ear. Irina would realize that she flew across the whole world to watch a gutter cat groom itself. That is, should she ever choose to get on the plane in the first place.

Today Irina's double is out somewhere in the great big world, unfindable. Irina reaches out to her the only way she knows how. She goes to a large, windowless department store like the ones they used to shop in together. She picks out a gauzy silk scarf, dark blue with golden curlicues. It feels like a breath passing between her fingers. She pays for it in cash. On the money she hands over to the salesclerk, she has written her message in tight black script, the unanswerable query she has for her friend she will never see again:

You know how to end things.
Tell me how to begin.

Acknowledgments

Special thanks to Bonnie Nadell for helping me flesh out the protagonist, Laura Tisdel for tightening a tentative manuscript into a lean book, Betsy Uhrig and Eleanor Beram for their untiring attention to detail.

Big thanks to Simona Necula for vetting the fairy tales, and to my writing group (Louise Aaronson, Catherine Alden, Natalie Baszile, Leah Griessman, Susi Jensen, Kathryn Ma, Bora Reed, Suzanne Wilsey) for their support.

Most of all, undying gratitude to Harris Shapiro, whose steadfast love keeps me sane.

About the Author

Elena Mauli Shapiro is the author of the novel *13, rue Thérèse.* She lives in the Bay Area with her husband.